# THE GALISTEO
# ESCARPMENT

Also by Douglas Atwill from Sunstone Press

*Why I Won't Be Going to Lunch Anymore*

# THE GALISTEO ESCARPMENT

## A Novel

## Douglas Atwill

For Bob K. from
Doug Atwill
(A gift from
Jim Atwill)

SUNSTONE
PRESS

SANTA FE

On the Cover: "Bend in the River, Galisteo" by Douglas Atwill.
Book design by Vicki Ahl

Sunstone books may be purchased for educational, business, or sales
promotional use. For information please write:
Special Markets Department, Sunstone Press,
P.O. Box 2321, Santa Fe, New Mexico 87504-2321.

---

Library of Congress Cataloging-in-Publication Data

Atwill, Douglas.
  The galisteo escarpment : a novel / by Douglas Atwill.
    p. cm.
  ISBN 978-0-86534-595-9 (softcover : alk. paper)
  1. Art teachers--Fiction. 2. Santa Fe (N.M.)--Fiction. I. Title.

PS3601.T85G36 2008
813'.6--dc22

                                        2007049799

Published in

**WWW.SUNSTONEPRESS.COM**
SUNSTONE PRESS / POST OFFICE BOX 2321 / SANTA FE, NM 87504-2321 /USA
(505) 988-4418 / ORDERS ONLY (800) 243-5644 / FAX (505) 988-1025

For Agnes and Mary Louise

# Preface

Behind an adobe wall near my house I have several piles of building materials, bricks of different sizes, quarried stones, river rocks, wooden lintels, short ends of vigas, a fireplace surround, a pair of shutters from Virginia, windows taken out of houses about to be demolished, doors of curious dimensions from the flea market and other oddities. The sensible man can leave them for what they are, happy stacks of like matter, but the obsessed man sees a house wanting to be realized, or a studio, or a pergola. The pieces ask him aloud to be brought together, knowing they will be greater combined than left apart. Cooks probably have the same fixation, unable to ignore the ripe peaches alone in their wicker basket, imagining the glory of the succulent pie appearing later in the day, unable to leave well enough alone.

When I shifted focus this summer from building to writing, the twenty-one stories I wrote a few years ago became so much construction fodder, peaches awaiting their fate. This character asked to be brought back, another came forward reluctantly, this incident needed expansion, that incident changed in its outcome and there was a setting in another story the perfect size to contain them all. Thus, this book is built from bricks that were laid up before, and if parts seem familiar, this is the reason.

Moreover, it may be a preference of mine, something deeply imbedded, to use materials that had a former life. I remember with rue a small house for sale near Grasse many years ago, a four room farm-house built with the stone blocks stolen from a nearby ruined temple, the Roman numerals and letters turned this way and that, an elaborate cornice piece squeezed without ceremony over a window. Roman stones relaid in the eighteenth century, waiting quietly for me. How could I have passed them up?

As the title indicates, Galisteo, New Mexico plays a part in this story. Dozens of painters have fallen under its spell, not so much the village as the whole basin surrounding it. It may not be such a queer thing to bond with a place, to take up its parts as you might the tresses or eyes of a human paramour, to be entranced by them. You see colors there like nowhere else; blazing yellow light; patterns of darkness, almost blackness, even at mid-day; clay-reds and the full spectrum of siennas; greens that walk all the way to orange; clouds that pick up speed as they cross overhead, then slow down thereafter, and vistas nearly to another country.

So Galisteo is the unfinished business, at least one of them, that concerns our man Bronson, the young man becoming a painter. The story takes him other places, distracts him, seduces him, but in the end he cannot ignore its multi-colored call.

# 1

# Beautifully Rendered

Neil Bronson woke when the first light started to glow across the horizon and he knew that the coming day would be clear, hot and still, a perfect day for painting outside. The secrets to French weather, particularly to the weather of Vaucluse, were clearer to him in this third month of the painting expedition. If the day started with a small breeze stirring in the branches outside his windows, he knew it would later blow a gale, and only heavy rocks on ropes could hold the easel from flying away down-wind. On the rare morning when it was cloudy at dawn, a thunderstorm could be counted upon to spoil the middle hours of a painting day, drenching the unfinished canvas and the painter alike. This day, however, would offer a long stretch of uninterrupted countryside painting. Neither breeze nor wisp of cloud marred the day's prospects.

"Sam, wake up," he said to the man who shared the room.

It was a small upstairs bedroom with wallpaper of faded tuberoses, stacks of canvases with their faces to the wall filled the spaces between the rustic furniture. The two casement windows looked into the top branches of a horse-chestnut tree in the adjoining garden, black birds raucously cavorting there in the early sun.

"Ummm." Sam rolled over and propped himself up on his elbows. His hair was as dark as Neil's was light. Both were in the twenties, short men by standards of their peers, but with long backs, good for lifting. If judgment had to be made, it would be that both were from stout, peasant stock, descendants from the cottage rather than the castle.

Neil said, "It's still and clear. No wind. A perfect day."

Sam made another wordless noise, acknowledging the day's attributes.

"I'll wait for you downstairs."

He strapped a new, white canvas onto his easel and shouldered the easel pack as he left. Their room was on the second floor of the Metropole Café, one of six rooms rented by the week. The café shared a common wall with garden of the cathedral in Gordes. A group of Gordesiens wearing identical black berets was already in place at the café downstairs, standing over their café noirs at the high bar. Smoke filled the room already replete with the decades of Gauloise aroma.

"What for the painter? The painter who will make Gordes famous," said the barman, acknowledging the talent of the upstairs resident.

"*Café au lait, s'il vous plait*," Neil said.

Despite the bartender's enthusiasm, acceptance came slowly in a town like Gordes and maybe never completely to these two young Americans on a quest perhaps done better by French sons with talent. How could foreigners know more about art than countrymen? France almost invented Art. The men at the bar nodded amiably to Neil as he sat down at one of the small tables, evidence of a progress, however slight, on the road to approval. The locals had noted the incredible zeal of his day-after-day work and it earned him marks. Zeal was a quality most young Americans lacked, but not this young artist with a new canvas each day.

It was still unthinkable for Neil and Sam to join the group at the bar; they lived according to a strict pecking order, old veterans of the wars at the top going down to a young farmer, a beneficiary of his father's recent death, at the bottom. There was no room for newcomers unless they made a space themselves.

Neil gave them a friendly nod from his table across the room. Sam joined him in a few minutes and he also gave to the bar crowd the ceremonial signal of a slightly dipped head.

He said to Neil as he sat down, "It's our very last painting today. Number thirty for each of us. What do you think of that?"

Neil said, "I'm ready to be done with it all. Maybe I've managed to paint two or three really good paintings. I should probably do a few more to make up for those experimental ones at the beginning."

"Absolutely not. The first thirty is what we agreed to, not the thirty most *brilliant* paintings."

With their morning coffee finished, the two men walked south on the road out of town. Gordes crowned a hill with tile-roofed stone buildings pushed right to the edge like eager children at cliff-side. For ancient defensive reasons, perhaps the fear of Phoenician pirates on inland sorties or of invading Greek philosophers with destructive new ideas and plans for temples, villages in this part of the Vaucluse were never sited in the valleys, where streams and groves abounded but danger lurked. Instead, the houses, shops, narrow streets, small parks, churches and government offices crowded together behind walls in the safety of a dry summit. Remnants of perimeter walls remained, but no longer the necessary ramparts for a safe life.

It was a steep downhill trip for the first kilometer. The road switched back and forth upon itself and straightened out on the plain below with poplars lining each side. Houses on the edge of town, added during the pacific decades of the Third Republic, were grander with gardens and walled potagers, more land between the houses. At the town limits, the buildings ended abruptly and the fields began in earnest.

Sam and Neil walked another two kilometers past olive groves and rows of lavender and wheat-fields to a flat place before another long descent to the village of Apt, its church dome ten kilometers distant, visible on the horizon. This morning was Sam's turn to choose the precise spot where they would paint. It would be a hundred feet away from the paved road on a dirt trail between two fields, the green of spring long replaced by crisp ochre grasses and leaves desiccated by a hot summer. The grasses crackled under their steps as they got settled and cicadas already had started their clicking.

Four months ago in London, Sam had the idea for this summer. They would paint thirty paintings in three months, a whole season in the Vaucluse with daily forays into the countryside, easels on their backs . It would be easy to do, Sam said, and a head-start on their careers in the art world now that the Royal Academy was safely behind them. They would find cheap rooms in a village and walk each day to the surrounding fields for whole days of the eternal, Vincentean struggle.

London had offered them the painting techniques of the modern and the politically correct, but not the sound grounding of *plein air* landscape. They could only discover that on their own. Only after thirty canvases had built up in stacks against the walls of their cheerless room would they quit, arms and noses burned brown. Thirty finished canvases each, that is.

As the actual summer progressed, Neil's paintings had become more personal, more domestic. He peered with more precision into the foreground, emphasized the parts of the landscape he could touch nearby and reduced the mid-ground and distance to bravura strokes of color, shapes of a single hue. The horizon in his paintings crept higher and higher on the canvas, sometimes cropping out the sky entirely.

On this new day's motif, he sketched in a study of grasses in the foreground, lightly drawing the distant dome at the top of the picture. The details of whatever lay between these two anchors would take up his entire day. While Neil's actual canvas size had become smaller, his paintings encompassed a larger scope, the faraway as well as the up-close.

Sam was quick to notice this strength in Neil's work and for the last weeks he came by for a look at his friend's easel more often, inspecting his growth with a keen interest. It was a gentle competition, but unrelenting, nonetheless. After the men had worked for an hour, Sam walked over to inspect Neil's take on their motif. He looked in silence for a long while, then said, "It's your best."

"I think so, too."

"Where did you start?"

"In the middle of the front this time, and then the edges and tops take care of themselves."

"Easy to say but hard to do. It's that maddening advice to every young sculptor to take away anything that's not needed."

Neil said, "I think I'm beginning to understand that."

"You must be, because it shows. Look at this. You went right into the heart of the scene, cropping everything else out. I'm impressed."

Neil wondered if Sam was annoyed at this improvement. Sam had always been the greater talent, and in school it was expected that Sam would produce a superior piece to whatever Neil had done. Sam could fill a large canvas with bold designs quickly, then integrate a filigree of pattern to make it all sing. Younger students lined the studio walls when he started a new piece. This interest by Sam of Neil's progress was something new in the balance between the two. For now, Neil put that idea on hold and returned to thinking about his own painting.

The temperature by early afternoon was hot. Neil, with a white kerchief around his head, walked over to Sam's easel to look over his canvas. Sam was a well-practiced artist and his canvas reflected that. Everything about it was academically correct, maybe just more than correct. The distant town of Apt sat stolidly on the horizon, expertly detailed, sunny sides of the buildings jumping out of the en-yellowed haze. The foreground was unfinished, sketchy lines only. Neil knew that his own work had soared above Sam's and it worried him to form comments that might not disparage his friend's painting.

"It's perfect, Sam. The town is beautifully rendered."

"It's okay, isn't it?"

"More than okay. It's your number thirty. We did it."

"Give me half an hour more," Sam said.

Today they had agreed to paint until two, when Carrie Ferrand, the third member of their summer sojourn, planned to pick them up in her auto and drive them to Apt for a late lunch. It would be a celebration lunch for the last of their thirty paintings. Carrie had graduated from the Royal Academy with them and was not to be left behind when they planned their summer, untypically acting as handmaiden to their efforts.

Neil unbolted his painting from the easel and folded the legs together, arranged the brushes and paints in the wooden case and closed it. He carried it all over to the shade of a nearby tree and propped the painting against the pack for viewing. The canvas was clearly his best of the summer, one of those where hand and mind worked together without conflict.

It was six hours since they started off from Gordes, the usual duration of their painting day. Neil worked faster than Sam, and was typically done when Sam needed another hour or so.

Sam had been the meteor of their academy years, earning highest marks in every pursuit and the admiration and envy of his fellow students. He was the one who would invade New York and have the critics at his feet, whimpering for more. The role of supporter and assistant came naturally to Neil; it was the enduring pattern of the relationship between the two men. Sam graciously allowed Neil to adore him, for which with equal grace Neil returned adoration. Offer the cheek, kiss the cheek. So this new twist of Neil's work being better than Sam's foretold a disturbing direction, a first blip on the balance of power between them. Beta male becoming alpha male, that was not supposed to happen.

The academy was a school for contemporary art where edgy, at the front-of-the-war, shells-dropping-around-you paintings were all that really mattered. Portrait painting, still-life, landscape or *contra-jour* compositions had no place there; it was as if they never even existed. Art schools at the time all downplayed the past, encouraging experiment and journeys into unknown lands.

The two men and Carrie spent many hours in the London museums, not always going straight to the modern wing. In secret, traitorous secret, they wondered what they were missing in the academy's total avoidance of what went before. Carrie was particularly taken with the portrait painters of the past, Sargeant, Whistler, and Velasquez. Both Sam and Neil went again and again to the 19th Century landscapists and the Impressionists, wondering if they could actually paint something as striking as a Monet, a Constable or a Turner. In their final week at the academy at the wine bar in Soho they had taken as their own, Sam suggested they teach themselves *plein air* painting, and it called for a trip to the South of France before they returned to the States. Thirty paintings would be enough to see if they had the touch. If they failed, they would at least have a nice, late-summer bonfire.

Neither Sam nor Neil had money to spare. Neil's family could well afford to send him more, but strongly believed they should not. In his undergraduate years, he drove a taxi and waited upon tables to pay the bills. There was a steel barrier between him and the family money, to be breeched only when Neil reached an inexact mature age. Early riches had spoiled other generations of Bronson men, turned them to drink and degradation, so the solution was simple: a very, very small allowance, regularly paid but never enlarged. If Bronsons did not starve in the streets, at least they would not be driving about in cloth-topped cars with adoring girls at their sides.

Sam's Boston family, eleven strong, could barely afford to pay for heat each winter. What they lacked in comfort was made up for in love, siblings working to support the education of the younger ones. Sam, without rancor and with boundless vigor, worked for everything in undergraduate school, and the academy stepped in to recognize his great promise with full scholarship.

Neil and Sam had already paid for their passages home on an Italian ship, the bottom deck stateroom, right over the propellers. They expected without question that they would fall quickly into work in New York on their return, perhaps waiting tables again or working in art galleries. They would paint at night or any extra time squeezed between work schedules until some gallery took up their cause. That they would be discovered and taken up on high was never doubted

Carrie, the beneficiary from her grandmother of a large trust fund, offered to pay the way for all three of them to their summer idyll in France, but both Neil and Sam felt uncomfortable with that. So the men rented a small room over the Metropole while Carrie had a two-room suite in the Auberge de Gordes on the other side of the cathedral. The three of them met every evening in small cafes and bars, looking at what the men had painted, critiquing each canvas as they had learned in London.

Sam was finally finished with his thirtieth painting.

"Voila. We've done it," he said.

They put together their easel packs and walked over to the road just at two o'clock. Carrie was seldom late.

# 2

# Buying Wholesale

Her black convertible stopped next to the two men and they loaded their packs into the back seat. Neil sat up front next to Carrie, and Sam climbed over into the seat behind with the easels. Carrie was taller by an inch than either of the men, slim, dressed in jeans and a blue silk blouse. Her blonde hair showed in wisps around the patterned scarf on her head.

"Before we leave, let me see what you've painted," she said.

Sam held his canvas up first. He had finished the foreground with a virtuoso zig-zag composition of grasses and native shrubs, taking the eye quickly back to highly worked details of the town on the horizon. Neil saw that his bold solution to the foreground had saved the painting from its commonplace beginning. Sam's ever present competitive spirit soared when he viewed Neil's work and it pushed him into a skillful solution. Neil was impressed, partly at the canvas itself and partly at the strength of the obsession that it evidenced.

"Now yours, Neil."

He retrieved his canvas from the top of the easel pack in the back seat. It was wet, so he handled it gingerly. Quite a bit smaller than Sam's painting, it nonetheless held the strength of design and color that Sam had seen earlier in the day. The town on the horizon was but a silhouette in dusty violet, no details such as windows and shadows whatsoever. It was, in fact, far less realistic than Sam's rendition. The reverse of Sam's, it brought the eye strongly forward, away from the horizon to the ably crafted rows of grasses, shadows and native plants. Neil's palette was more daring, with the strong colors of the Fauves, an orange in the shadows, black in the outlines and a Chinese red in unexpected places.

Sam asked, "Well? Who wins?"

"You two always want me to choose. I love you both and think you're both brilliant," Carrie said. She was not about to start a battle between the two men. It amused Sam to bring them to the precipice of choice, but Carrie always avoided falling over it.

She changed the subject with, "Anyway, I have a dazzling plan. It involves all of your paintings and your future in New York this fall." She started the engine, tightened the knot of her scarf and pulled back onto the road, quickly accelerating in the direction of Apt. Neither of the two men knew what to make of her statement, but without looking at one another, they thought better of asking for clarity at this time. Carrie proceeded on her own clock, and they knew it was futile to slow it down or speed it up.

Sam said, "So we'll hear about this plan soon?"

"Soon."

They drove in silence the rest of the way. The breeze was a welcome change from the still, hot afternoon. It had been many weeks since rain or a single cloud of any promise. The fields had dried to ochre yellow and sienna, interspersed with the dusty, gray foliage of the olive groves. Goats and sheep huddled together in the scant shade. The Vaucluse seemed to be waiting for the end of summer, silent and hot, with skies of a deep, chemical blue, no breeze stirring a single branch.

She drove into the village centre and found parking on a side street. They locked their easel-packs and canvases in the trunk and set off for the café.

She said, "I've asked Nicole to join us. I know that you don't particularly like her, but I ask you to be civil. She's been a good friend to me while the two of you were off on your countryside obsessions. She shopped today for antiques in Perget and will join us when she's done."

Nicole Bertralle owned the inn where Carrie had rooms. Nicole inherited the inn when her father died ten years ago and she had refurbished the ten lackluster rooms with antiques she bought in neighboring villages and trips to the *Marche aux Puces* in Paris. Each year of her proprietorship saw a finer polish on things, an upgrading of quality. She found a talented woman chef for the small restaurant attached to the inn and customers now traveled the hour's trip from Avignon just for lunch. Summer guests had a half pension from a special menu, dishes not often seen outside Paris. The Auberge de Gordes was getting good notice in the travel guides and Paris reviews. Vacant rooms were scarce this summer, but Nicole rescheduled several early reservations to give Carrie a full summer there.

Neil said, "It's not that we don't like her. We hate her."

Sam joined in with, "When the two of you are talk in French and laugh, with that knowing look our way, why wouldn't we be touchy?"

She said, "At least be civil for one of our last lunches together. Please?"

It was true that the two men did not care for Nicole, mostly because she seemed to siphon off the attention that Carrie had formerly reserved exclusively for them. They had been happy in the glow of Carrie's sun and an eclipse by Nicole brought only a coolness and a darkness.

Carrie led them to a small wine bar next to the church and ordered them a pitcher of white wine. She took off her scarf, shook out her hair and poured a glass for each of them as she said, "Now, my brilliant idea about your future. Your joint futures, I should say."

Sam said, "Good, I hope it involves money, because when we get to New York I will be down to five cents.

"Me, too," Neil said.

"The idea is inspired, I think. It does involve money. I will take your sixty paintings back to London and organize an exhibit at Hetty's gallery in Dover Street. You remember her. She owes me big-time for the dozen or so paintings my father bought there. When he stayed at Brown's, which was often, I took him over to her gallery and guided him through the niceties of buying a painting. He bought several he did not like because of me."

Sam said, "But why would she want to exhibit our paintings?"

"Your paintings are accomplished, particularly the later ones, and they will sell quickly, I am sure. The sales would give you both a nest egg for New York. Hetty Sloan is a dedicated traditionalist, but also down deep a true English shop-keeper and she likes anything so long as it sells. Then, you won't need to wait tables in Tribeca or work in gallery back rooms to make ends meet."

"I don't think it's as simple as that, Carrie," Neil said.

"Of course, it is."

Sam said, "I wonder about Hetty's gallery, though. She specializes in nineteenth century work. Big bouquets and bowls of fruit. Thoroughbred horses in front of country houses. Long-toothed women in period dress, colors too strong for their English complexions. I swear on her sign it says right under her name: Paintings of the Deceased British Academicians from the nineteenth century."

"That's almost right," Carrie said. "But your paintings of the South of France will give her a new look, something to attract the old pussies of both genders who stay at Brown's Hotel. Contemporary landscapes are not that far afield. I know it will work. I am sure she will agree."

"They are good, aren't they," Sam asked, more of a statement than a question.

"Absolutely. Let me call her tonight."

Neil said, "It's okay by me. Let's do it."

"Splendid. You won't regret it," she said.

He continued, "I do have something else to bring up to the two of you, as well. Since we are in fact done with our project and the summer isn't over yet, why don't we spend a few weeks somewhere on the coast? Sam can drive us in your car."

"Our very own water nymph. Always wanting to go to the seashore," Carrie said.

"It's true, I confess. No summer seems right without a dip into the sea. The Mediterranean holds a fascination for me, its the very water that Odysseus, Tiberius and Madame Matisse all swam about in, if not together."

Sam said, "Our ship home from Genoa isn't until September so I'll say yes to both propositions. It will have to be a very cheap place as I have only three hundred or so left. Do you think Hetty could send us a small advance?"

Carrie said, "Don't push it, Sam. I'll call her tonight."

Nicole found them in the wine bar. She pulled up an extra chair, and they started to pour her a glass of wine. She put her hand over the glass. "I had a good morning in Perget. My old friend there has been raiding his family chateau again, his mother away in Paris for a month. Four eighteenth century rush seated chairs and a Regénce bureau plat. I'm starved for lunch. *Allons.*"

She led them next door to the café and expertly secured a table under the awning against the front wall, cool but fully open to street-side. The waiter was instantly there, sensing the no-nonsense power that Nicole exuded in public. She ordered, without consulting the other three, four of the daily special *dejeuners* for the all of them, raising her eyebrows for tacit approval. If Neil and Sam gave in, it was only on the surface, for a moment's peaceful retreat.

Nicole was a dark-haired version of Carrie, slim and casually dressed in jeans, a black silk blouse and large straw hat. She was a few years older than Carrie, but her youthful demeanor gave her an air of a school-mate.

Carrie said, "We've much to celebrate. Neil and Sam's sixty paintings are completed. An exhibit in London arranged, well, *almost* arranged. And we have just come up with a trip to the Riviera for a couple of weeks of sea-water. Will you join us for some swimming and sunning, Nicole?"

"No, no. It's much too busy now in Gordes. Maybe in October."

Sam said, "But you won't have our glorious company in October, Nicole. Handsome American men with stunning bodies frolicking in the waves. It will make you insane with desire."

"Ah, yes. But imagination must suffice."

Carrie asked, "Where should we stay, Nicole? August will be crowded I know, and we are definitely on a budget."

"I may have just the thing. My uncle in his will left me his summer house in Cabasson-sur-Mer. Not the Riviera, closer to Marseilles. It's very simple fisherman's house, but on the edge of town. Applewood tables, chairs that lean, dishes that don't match. The Paris family that always rents it for August has cancelled. Most annoying. Perhaps you would like to rent it? It's available starting tomorrow."

"How much for two whole weeks?" Sam said.

"Five thousand francs."

"Ouch. I was hoping for something around eight hundred francs."

Nicole's expression indicated her displeasure. "It is High Season for rents and my uncle did not leave it to me just for me to give it away. It is a big part of my annual income. I am not a charitable association." Despite her youthful and modern demeanor, underneath Nicole was truly French.

Neil said, "Cool down, I guess we'll look farther down the coast. Maybe that's what the Paris family did, too."

Nicole scowled at him. She said, "You make fun, but rents are what feed me. I have no talents like all of you. I must use what my family gives me."

Carrie said, "I have an idea. Another dazzler." She paused to get their attention. "What if Nicole took a painting in trade from each of you for three weeks rent on her uncle's house? She just yesterday said how she admired the work of yours she had seen and both of you want proper remuneration for your talent."

She turned to Nicole and said, "There are plans for an exhibit of these paintings in London, at a gallery just across from Brown's Hotel. I am sure their prices will go up handsomely and easily make up your loss of rent." Carrie, as well as Nicole, had some merchant genes in her make-up that popped into existence at surprising times. Buying at wholesale was part of the gene pool.

"Her choice of paintings?" Sam asked.

"My choice, of course," Nicole said, smiling.

"No, *my* choice," Carrie said.

Nicole took a drink of water and considered it. Neil thought he could almost hear gears moving around in her head; maybe she was a French cyborg, a mobile adding machine made in a secret factory on the coast. Not looking directly at them, she finally said, *"D'accord."*

Sam watched Neil's face for approval. They all nodded agreement and clinked wine-glasses. The meal proceeded without further mention of rentals or paintings. Carrie paid the bill for all of them and they walked away in the direction of their cars.

Nicole said, "Oh, Neil, I almost forgot. Your mother called from the States this morning at the Auberge. She could not get past the public telephone in the bar at the Metropole, even though she has very good French."

"She went to school in Switzerland as a girl. Henri at the bar has his strict orders from Madame. No telephone for the room renters. What did my mother want?"

"You must call her immediately. Not life or death, but *très important*, she said."

Neil knew that his mother missed talking to him, sharing family news and hearing about his adventures. She had called several times a week during his years in London, involving him in every family crisis, however small. The barrier of the local phone at the Metropole was thwarting her connection with her favorite offspring. At least, so far.

"Margaret can wait until we get back from the seashore. It's only *tres important*, after all, not urgent or earth-shaking," he said.

# 3

# A Kilo of Figs

It was a day's drive from Gordes to Cabasson-sur-Mer, the vineyards and orchards merging into wheatfields, and finally through the fragrant pine forests along the coast, down the steep cliffs to the beachside. Sam drove most of the way as he was the acknowledged best driver of the three and the most eager to actually drive. Neil took the wheel for a spell through Aix-en-Provence and beyond, but Sam stepped in again to bring them down the narrow road into Cabasson just at sunset.

They found Nicole's house with the town map that she provided and parked on the street in front of it. Neil took the key and opened the door. The captured smell of cooking herbs and seaside damp was strong, filling the still air of the closed house. It was as Nicole had described, very simple. A stone cottage, white-washed inside and out, with a ceiling of dark beams and mismatched, country furniture in every room. Two bedrooms, each with twin beds and a bathroom at the end of the hall. The rest of the house was a single large room, which served as a kitchen, dining and sitting area. Neil opened the door to the walled garden in the back, the source of the strong cooking herbs. A rampant fig tree filled one corner of the garden with a sharp-thorned sour orange in the other, perennial herbs standing tall in between.

After they got settled, Carrie in one room and the two men in the other, she said, "Let's walk down to the village before it gets dark and get dinner."

As they explored the sloping streets, Neil said, "By the way, I suppose you will choose for Nicole the two very best paintings of our show. You might pick two of our early ones, instead."

"No. I didn't. She deserves your best work, but maybe not the *very* best. They were the second-best out of sixty."

"Second best? Did you do that on purpose?"

"Yes, because of personal reasons."

"And those are...?"

"Both of you are running out of money, I know. I also know that you would not accept a loan from me, as you never have before. Foolish male pride."

"Just because we have a rich friend doesn't mean we should take advantage of her," Sam said.

"I know, I know. But what is the use of having some extra money if I can't occasionally make life easier for the ones I love?"

"We just couldn't, Carrie."

"That's why I am going to *buy* a painting from each of you. If Nicole can profit from your talent, then it seems only fair that your best friend should, too. So I selfishly reserved the crème-de-la-crème for myself."

The two men remained silent.

Carrie continued, "Mind you, I'm not paying Hetty's London prices. Five hundred dollars each."

"That's too generous," Sam said, looking for Neil's approval. "Besides, I am not sure that we really want to sell them."

"It's only right that you let me buy them. There is fair value for me there, so don't let egos get in the way of a great arrangement for both sides."

She handed them both an envelope. "Here it is in francs. I didn't want our stay here to be spoiled with your worries about money, when there's an easy solution." The two men took the envelopes with reluctant expressions.

"So which ones did you choose?" Neil asked.

"I will show you when we get back."

They walked into the town center, a semi-circle of three-storied buildings that fronted onto the harbor, lined with fishing boats in their night dock. A stone quay in front of the buildings was barely wide enough for the neat rows of white-clothed tables of three cafes. The early evening promenade was in full bloom, citizens walking back and forth slowly, chatting with neighbors, squeezing single file past the bulge of café tables at the risk of a plunge into the water. The was no breeze to cool off the day's heat.

They chose the café in the middle and seated themselves at a table midway back. Neil had a fixed smile, a man in heaven, as they watched the dusk over the small harbor. It was as perfect as he had hoped. The other parts of the southern coast had grown into an urban sprawl many years before, with high rise apartment blocks crowding the view and destroying the waterside ambiance of the old fishing villages. Cabasson-sur-Mer was one of those overlooked in the rush to develop villas and apartments on every sea-view acre. The fishing boats went out each day from the harbor and returned with catch in the evening. A citizen could still buy hardware, canned goods and bolts of striped cotton from shops opening on the quay. Cabasson had not ceded its village center yet to tourist shops and galleries.

When the waterside meal had been cleared away and they sat with espressos, Carrie said, "I am almost afraid of the future, you know."

Sam asked, "Afraid of going home, back to the States?"

"No. Fearful of changing what has become a pattern of the three of us together. How can that survive back home?"

Neil said, "Maybe it can."

She replied, "How can it? Both of you in New York, art careers, fame. I will get all the pressure from my father to get married, to 'settle down.'"

The two carafes of wine were taking hold as Sam said, "Since I love both of you I can't image that we won't be together always."

Neil looked at Sam for a long time, then stood up to start their departure. They walked slowly up the hill to the house.

The next day Neil rose early, before the other two, and explored both sides of the town, choosing the beach just to the west of the harbor for their day of sun and water. He took an early swim as the sun was rising, the sea still cool from the night. It was clear and green, easily revealing the pebbly bottom at forty feet from shore. He swam quickly out far enough to see the harbor around the promontory rocks, then in a slow float came back to the shore. He ran up the carved steps in the beach cliff and up the road to Nicole's house, still dripping.

"Get up. Get up. Paradise beckons not a quarter mile away."

Carrie was up already and had made coffee. Sam was still asleep. She said, "Three weeks doing nothing. Swimming. Reading. No painting."

"I can't promise I won't paint. I want to start on some edge-of-the-water scenes."

"Maybe we should have come here first instead of Gordes."

"No. Gordes gave us our summer's project, however dry and hot it was. I'll always be the thankful for that, those ochre colors and pale horizons. They're imprinted on my mind now, part of my being. But I feel that somewhere on the Mediterranean could be a house, a cottage or a villa waiting for me. Not Nicole's house, but somewhere else. Not for right now, but in a time after we get settled in New York."

"Why do you think that?"

"I know it, deep within me."

She said, "Do you think you lived here before, in another lifetime?"

"Reincarnation is such poppycock. However, it could explain why it resounds with me so solidly. Pacific and Atlantic shores do nothing for me, compared to this. The North Sea is too cold, the Caribbean too hot. The Mediterranean has the quality of being just right. Ten thousand years of civilization might say so, too. Why should one place exert such a deep personal attraction if your past was not in some way linked with it?"

After their late breakfast at one of the cafes on the quay, they provisioned Carrie's basket with white wine and cheese, a loaf of bread, grapes and a kilo of ripe figs. Neil showed them the way to his newly discovered beach. Large granitic rocks protected both ends, no more than 100 feet apart and a low bluff made the back wall, with steps cut out of solid rock from the road above. Instead of sand, it had a beach of very small pebbles which felt cool on the feet. There was no surf, only a slight lapping of the water, and it was five minutes from their cottage. Cabasson-sur-Mer had been waiting for them, Neil thought, maybe for centuries.

Their first day there was idyllic from beginning to end. The beach was virtually empty all day, with only a short incursion by a group of boys cascading over the end rocks into the still waters, splashing, yelling, and laughing.

Carrie was a strong swimmer and went far out on her own, while Neil and Sam watched from their beach towels. She turned and waved back several times as she swam. Neil looked at Sam and asked, "Could you live a life here? Days and nights on *Mare Nostrum*? I think I could be very happy here."

"I don't think I could. I'm the city boy who understands subways and skyscrapers. New York. High-end galleries. Art museums. The world of art and artists that we've always talked about."

"But what about in our off-time? Summers and holidays?"

"Maybe, but for a while there won't be much off-time and no holidays. I grant you, it should appeal to me more since I'm Italian, and they all like the Mediterranean, but somehow it doesn't. Maybe I'm not really Italian, a spawn from my mother's Polish lover."

"Sam, I want you in my life always."

Sam turned and looked at Neil, aware that Neil's talk had gone to deeper waters.

"Me, too. Why won't I be there? You're just as interested in New York as I am, maybe more so. What's this suddenly about the Mediterranean?"

Neil didn't respond directly, but said, "I can see you getting married, having a family. The famous artist with an adoring wife, flotilla of kids, news cameras flashing at the household artistic, the envy of every East Coast male. There wouldn't be a place for me."

"That is not even in the near future, much more like years down the line. We have the New York world of art to conquer, bud. Besides, even though you're not big with the ladies, you could find a wife and have kids, too."

"I don't think that's going to happen, Sam."

"Maybe so." He rolled over and put his hand on Neil's shoulder. "Don't worry, you'll always be mine, Neil." Sam knew what Neil wanted to hear, however faint the chances were.

The week inched along through days of water and sun, dinners on the harbor front and occasional meals at home in the garden of salad and fish in Nicole's cottage. Neil started to paint a few hours each day, setting up his easel on the rocks above their beach. Sam and Carrie fell into the complete torpor of summer heat with long naps in the afternoon, late awakenings in the morning. If Neil got up and out early, the two others gave into the languor of the ancient coast.

# 4

# Thirty-Two Thousand

In the rocks above the beach, if there were still alive a few of the provincial Roman gods, the ones who could grant a cloudless day and still waters for a shallow promise and a handful of wildflowers, they made themselves known that week. Each day broke with a golden peach light and progressed unsullied, cloudless and perfect until the sun, pomegranate red, dipped back into night behind the pines and villas on the far promontory. The exquisite torpor of a Mediterranean summer had trapped them entirely.

It was four in the afternoon in the middle of their second week at Cabasson. The days on the beach and evenings at the harbor cafes were too full for them, too touching on perfection to consider even so much as short venture along the coast to other beaches, other harbor villages. The two men became deeply tanned, but Carrie, despite her love of swimming, stayed out of the sun mostly, in the shade of an umbrella next her supine men.

Carrie noticed how deeply tactile Sam was. He made a point in conversation with Carrie by stroking her arm or pulling his knees against her side. She watched as he lay in the sun with arm over Neil's chest or back. His favorite position was face-down on the towel, his head in an opposite direction from the others with one hand on Neil's right foot and the other on Carrie's left foot. If she moved ever so slightly, Sam would grip tighter. Did he think they would disappear from his life if he did not hold on and hold on tightly?

The warm feel of Neil's hand on her shoulder or the brush of his cheek against her face was what she really wanted, but Neil was not as quick to touch. She thought how amused the Gods must be with the three of them, how omnipresent the Olympians seemed to be here in their home waters. She loved Neil, Neil loved Sam and Sam loved her. It was summer dance only the Old Ones could have arranged, gleeful at the sharp corners of the triangle, corners that could smart when brushed against.

The silence was broken by the sound of a car coming to a stop on the gravel above the bluff. An older woman in a red blouse and white slacks, and large-brimmed straw hat of matching red, got out of the car and started uneasily down the uneven steps. Carrie wondered if the woman would fall off the steps, but she made it, racing down the last steps to the bottom with arms outstretched for balance. She walked directly towards them. Neil and Sam were asleep as she approached.

"May I share your beach umbrella?" she whispered to Carrie.

"Yes, of course."

The woman sat down gracefully in the umbrella's shade and took off the large hat. Her hair was a well-tended blonde, once natural but now with salon assistance, pulled back into a sizeable chignon. Not a single golden strand escaped this fashionable stricture. In the red straw bag that matched her hat, she found a cigarette, lit it and inserted it expertly into a tortoise-shell holder.

"I'm Margaret, Neil's mother."

Carrie said, "What a surprise. How did you find us?"

"The young girl at the café thought you would be down here, after I gave her a large tip. Also, your friend Nicole provided me with excellent directions out of Gordes. I like her, by the way. A stylish, smart woman."

"Yes, of course."

"My son has been avoiding me, so I've rather taken matters in hand, come over to France to settle things. A woman needs the mind of a spy, especially a mother."

"I'd better wake him."

Neil, hearing their conversation, awoke on his own, turned over slowly and when he saw his mother, jolted upright.

"Margaret, good god." He stood up, brushed the sand off his chest and leaned down to kiss her on the offered cheek.

"The strength of mother-love has no bounds." She drew a long puff on her cigarette.

"I'm sorry, Margaret. Events pressed in, and we got too busy to answer your call. I was going to telephone when we got back to Gordes." But he knew her sudden appearance was not just about his avoidance of returned telephone calls. Something else loomed.

"It couldn't wait that long, my dear."

"So, what is it?"

"Now that I've found you, I'm going to make *you* wait until tonight. Nicole told me that you made a joke of my urgency, as if 'très important' had no meaning. Mother doesn't like being made fun of. I assume that is Sam sleeping over there and you must be Carrie." Carrie nodded.

Neil asked, "Is it about Dad? Is he okay?"

"No, he's fine. I'll buy dinner for the three of you at my hotel tonight, the Eden Roc down the coast. Come at eight." She got up and walked slowly back up to the car. With a screech of gravel, she was off down the road.

Carrie looked at Neil expectantly. "What do you think has happened?"

"Margaret has a keen sense of the dramatic. It could be anything, even something insignificant, but I have a feeling it's something significant."

The calm pattern of their day had been shattered. Much as they hoped to mend it, after a desultory swim they gave in and went to the cottage to get ready for the dinner at Eden Roc.

The hotel was ten miles to the east on a long promontory, a *faux* Moroccan village of white-washed domes, cottages, palm trees and a staff with curled-toe shoes. Pulling into the long entrance drive, they allowed a turbaned footman to park the car, while they crossed the large lobby to the bar. Neil could hear Margaret's laugh across the lobby, above the sounds of the jazz group.

She sat on one of the stools at the bar, talking to the barman and a stranger on the stool next to her. She waved to the three and motioned them to take a far table in the otherwise empty lounge. Her conversation with the two men continued for a few minutes, and then she joined them.

"Let's get all your drink orders," she said. The barman obliged.

"Margaret, you look fantastic, as usual," Neil said.

"Thank you, dear. A little pulling up, only."

"So, I can't wait. What is so important you've come all the way to France?"

"I have a letter here. It's from your Uncle Lionel. I'll let you read it and then the two of your must also read it." She handed Neil a sealed envelope.

"By way of explanation to Carrie and Sam. Lionel is my older brother. He is the owner and headmaster of a School of Art in Santa Fe. Also my favorite family member. There are interesting troubles at the school and I'm here on his behalf."

Neil opened the envelope and it read:

*Dear Nephew:*

*Circumstances require me to ask an enormous favor, to humble myself deeply and ask that you come immediately to my rescue. The Monmouth clan has always clustered together in time of danger and we must circle now, all Scotland ablaze with kilts akimbo and swords sharpened.*

*Events have conspired to produce good fortune for Lionel Monmouth School of Art, not, I must add, without results. Two of my former students, a Mr. Brendt Basse-Noir and a Miss Martha Noggidge, were interviewed this January by The New York Times, featuring their meteoric rise in the New York world of art. Each now earns a handsome sum annually from their endeavors. They were good, but not excellent students of my school.*

*You are ahead of me here, I know. They gave the Monmouth School and me, personally, credit for their spectacular rise, giving my small enterprise the dazzling light of notoriety. Instead of the usual half a dozen applications for new students this spring, I have received over fifty for the fall term. Alas, most of the applicants seem qualified, having completed their undergraduate time with honors.*

*With some expansions and revisions, I might be able to accommodate forty new students for the term starting this September. We are refurbishing the old studios here, finding accommodation in the town for most of them. You'll remember Miss Louisa Marriner, my aide-de-camp, who is rallying everybody together for this onslaught.*

*This is where you and Sam come into the scenario. With both of you holding Masters of Arts Cum Laude from the Royal Academy, you are well qualified by any measure to teach art in an American school. I implore both of you to come to Santa Fe for a year, at salaries of $32,000 and teach* at the Monmouth School. It would vastly aid your beleagured uncle and you would be young stars in my firmament. We will discuss details after you have indicated your assent to Margaret, who has graciously agreed to hand deliver this and record your reponse..

I well know that both of you consider Santa Fe a stale backwater in the world of Art, justly forgotten in the currents that really matter, and that you have your hearts set on New York. One year set aside before that quest would pull your Monmouth family out of its dilemma and it could strengthen your hand in the onslaught of Gotham. I implore you both.

Respond immediately, love
Lionel.


Neil said on finishing the letter, "Margaret, this isn't fair."

"Let Sam and Carrie read it and we'll talk."

Carrie read it first and then Sam. Margaret ordered more drinks for everybody and then they were set to talk about it.

"I'll say again, Margaret, this just isn't fair. You know I've had my heart set on going to New York and so has Sam."

"It would help Lionel enormously and it would make your mother happy."

Neil continued, "And that bit about the Monmouth clan in their kilts clustered together in time of Low-land danger has the sound of you, not Lionel."

"Guilty, I must say. I thought it might insert a tone of gravitas to the letter if we had to send it in the mail. But it is a subject not without merit. Your family *does* need help and it's only fair, considering what the family has done for you over the years, that you return it in kind."

"No, Margaret. I remember those summers with Lionel. Santa Fe is a Podunk backwater with mostly third-rate painters posing as important and grand. It will never be on the edge of art."

She turned to Sam, "What do you think, Sam? Just one year in Santa Fe, which heaven knows is *not* a backwater dump but an important, international-artist conclave. You could save most of your salary and it would give you a year of living expenses in the bank before you go to New York."

"It makes sense, Mrs. Bronson, but if Neil doesn't like it...."

Neil interrupted, "Besides, Carrie is not mentioned in the letter at all. She has a degree, as well, and we were planning to stay together this next year."

"I am sure Lionel can find a place for Carrie, as well."

They went into dinner and tried to discuss other things. Margaret steered the conversation to the Cote d'Azur, criminal overdevelopment, but her heart was not in persiflage. She turned to Carrie for her next assault.

"Carrie, my dear, would you take a teaching position at the Monmouth School? Wouldn't it be a good way to get armed for the art career you all want eventually in New York?"

"Mrs. Bronson, I couldn't if Neil is against it."

Margaret said, "Ah, well, Neil. *Son.* It's up to you. Surely a short year out of a long life, and the Monmouths gave you the great advantage of longevity as well, would not be too much to ask. Think how fast the last year has passed. You would be in Soho or Tribeca before you know it, doing whatever it is you can't do in Santa Fe."

Sam had been quiet until now. "Maybe your mother is right, Neil. When these last five hundred dollars are gone, that's it. We each have thirty landscape paintings, correction: twenty-eight, as our sole assets. There certainly is a chance that the exhibit in London won't materialize or if it does, that we don't sell as many pictures as Carrie anticipates. Waiting on tables in New York is okay, and it's what I've always planned. But why, if we don't have to? *Thirty-two thousand.*"

Neil said, "I still say no. Life is too short, despite the alleged Monmouth longevity, to take detours here and there. And people have a way of getting stuck in the sand in Santa Fe, not going on to their potential."

Sam said, "But we would all be there together. And maybe we could learn something in the teaching of art for a year. It never entered my mind before, but I am sure we would have time to work on our own paintings, a portfolio to show to New York galleries. I think we should say yes."

Carrie nodded her assent, looking guiltily at Neil. He realized that the tide had turned on him and he certainly did not want to be in New York without Sam and Carrie. He could scarcely go on there alone and let the two of them help his own uncle two thousand miles away.

"Okay, Margaret, I give in." Neil thought of the dozens of other times he had said the same thing, the dutiful child.

"You always were a good boy, giving into mama's wishes."

"Don't push it, Margaret. I agree, but I have some requests, no, demands, before this can take place. First, we all have houses, nice houses, provided for us so we can, in fact, save our salaries for New York. And there will be separate studios for each of us."

Margaret said, "I have been given authority to offer whatever it takes. I think that your housing was understood, but I will clarify that with Lionel. The Casa Marriner is a huge compound, you know, with many back buildings and unused parlors."

"Also, you won't just 'find a place' for Carrie, you will offer her exactly the same position and salary as Sam and me."

"Done, of course."

"And I get to teach *plein air* painting. After this summer at Gordes, it interests me more than I would have thought."

"Also, done. What will you teach, Carrie?"

"I don't really know at this time. Something about modernism and O'Keeffe, I suppose. Feminist Art in the twentieth century. The Small Painting and Modernism, how does that sound?"

"And Sam?"

"If they have studio courses, I would like to take on those. Studio Workshop with Professor Bonifacio. "

"I am sure Lionel will be delighted with all of this."

With that, Margaret went to the front desk to make arrangements for her flight home. She kissed Neil and shook hands with the other two. The dinner and the interview were over, but the others stayed on to finish the wine.

Sam said, "I wonder of the State Department knows about her. She could make a difference in the Middle East."

"And the two of you dare question the power of women," Carrie said.

"I learned as a boy to just step aside when Margaret wanted something. It just wasn't worth the bruises to oppose her. So we are all going to Santa Fe."

# 5

# Wood Over Water

"Hello, Hetty, is that you?" Carrie said.

"Yes, love. How good to hear from you."

"Hetty, I have a favor to ask."

"Of course. *Anything*. Is your dear father coming to London again?"

"Not now. Perhaps this winter."

"So, what is the favor?"

"Something quite different."

Moments later Carrie had expertly trapped Hetty into sponsoring the exhibit. The gallery was booked solidly for most of the winter, she said, but there was an open week in early December. It would be for only seven days, as the very saleable estate of a long dead 19th Century Mannerist portraitist would fill the gallery over the holidays.

Carrie said, "And if you will have the paintings properly framed in London, you can send the bill to me."

"I can do that. Neil and Sam are very lucky to have you on their side."

"I think you'll be excited by the paintings"

"I sincerely hope so. And, by the way, your father *must* look in on his next stay at Brown's."

Carrie heard the implied contract in Hetty's voice. "I can assure it, Hetty."

The summer was finally over. Neil and Sam said goodbye to the denizens of the Metropole Bar after a full display of the summer paintings. If the fervor of their project had not impressed the men, the paintings themselves did. Nobody, however, offered to buy one, but there were many offerings of *bonne chance* and *aux revoir*.

Sam found two crates behind the bar that would hold the paintings; he wrapped them individually in paper and nailed the crates shut with a borrowed hammer. After they had loaded up the crates and luggage, Carrie drove Neil and Sam to Avignon to catch the evening train to Genoa. They went early to deliver the crates to the shippers in the train station.

There were several hours before departure so Carrie found parking beside the train station near the town centre. "Let's walk around a bit," she said.

The men checked their bags and the three of them walked through the leafy streets of old Avignon. Sam held hands with Carrie for a while. They stopped in a small park, savoring the hot stillness of the finale of their Provencal summer.

Carrie said, "Hetty will be delighted, once she doesn't feel so put-upon."

Sam said, "I was adding up what we might get if the paintings sold, and we're better off taking your Uncle Lionel's offer. I was figuring a forty percent gallery commission, minus framing and shipping."

Neil: "No one ever promised that the *plein air* landscapist's life was a rich one."

Sam: "Maybe Monet's was, toward the end."

Carrie: "Yours will be, I know."

As they walked back to the station, Sam said, "You can still book on the *S. S. Bellini* with us, Carrie. It wouldn't have to be steerage like me and Sam. Ten days to New York, with a stop in Sicily and Tangiers. We'd have fun."

"Thanks, but no."

"So you're definitely staying on in Gordes for a while?"

"I told Nicole I would. She thinks I give too much attention to the two of you. She wanted time for us, one-on-one."

"I'll bet."

"We'll have plenty of time together in Santa Fe."

Sam said, "I'm going to miss you, Carrie."

"I know."

"And I will, too," Neil said. "I've been thinking about Santa Fe. Maybe it's not as bad an idea as I thought originally. We will be, in fact, more prepared for New York. And certainly we'll have more money. Sam and me, that is. I'm glad the two of you convinced me to change my mind."

Sam said, "I think Nicole has her eye on you, Carrie. Be careful."

"She's just a friend, Sam. Not what you're implying."

"These French have a way of turning your head, Carrie. It's something in the air here in the South. I've even been looking at Neil in a different way." He looked at Neil in an exaggeratedly different way.

She said, "Stop. Get on your train."

The two men hugged and kissed Carrie in turn, then headed for the departure gate. It was a six hour train trip to Genoa with the ship waiting to sail at sunset. They arrived on time and took a taxi to the pier. Their cabin was the least expensive, at the starboard rear, next to the engine noise. The two Italian men who would share their cabin were already on the bunks, asleep.

Sam and Neil went up to the rear deck for the departure from the Genoa harbor. The ship left without tugboats, turning gracefully to the south and rose to full cruising speed as the lights of Genoa disappeared in the darkness.

The insistence hum of the engines and gurgling of the prop were like a lullaby for the two men, and they slept soundly, ignoring the Italian snores. Late the next morning, they were in Palermo, already docked at the Corso di Mare when they finished breakfast.

They had the day ashore. The old town with its congested streets and four-story buildings started right up from the docks. They walked up to the main piazza with the cathedral, dark with centuries of candle smoke. After several hours of the tightly packed streets, Neil suggested they get a ride to the countryside to get some air.

A man with a horse-drawn carriage was more than willing to take them for a few dollars, promising to be back by mid-afternoon. The city gave itself up grudgingly in zones of small factories and farms until they turned onto a back road leading right into peach and citrus orchards. Neil immediately felt better, putting aside the oppressive crush of Palermo's streets. Rain squalls from the sea rushed low over the island, but spared the carriage. They drove on past farms for several miles to a peninsula which ended at the parking court for an imposing villa, now converted to a hotel.

The lobby and the adjoining salons, all heavily furnished with Italian Art Nouveau, were dark and empty. The French doors opened onto a terrace with a stone wall above the sea and a view back to Palermo.

Sitting on the wall, Sam said, "So you want to live here on the Mediterranean in your heart of hearts."

"I do. I think I know why."

"Because you search for sensuous, irresistible Italians like me, that's why."

"That's true, but not the real reason. There is a quality of being primordial here, adjacent to the very beginnings of everything civilized. I don't get that in America. This nurtures the soul."

"How would you live here?"

"I don't see myself living here full time, but I can imagine having a bolt hole somewhere just above the water. A simple house with a walled garden. Old fruit trees and a grape-covered arbor to fend off the summer sun."

"Are you putting too much imagination to work? Asking too much?"

"I don't think so. My grandmother Monmouth had a terrace covered with grapes and she made lunches for me and my cousins there. She gave us sliced figs from her own tree and she even peeled our grapes. Maybe it's all a memory of that. "

"Is that your mother's mother?"

"She was Margaret and Lionel's mother. I know now she was what they call a white witch with certain small powers. If she couldn't exactly turn people into cats or frogs, she did see many things that others did not. She believed in omens and signs absolutely. I think I do, too."

"You're a hopeless romantic, through and through, aren't you?"

"Does that mean I give in to the heart before the mind?"

"I think so. It may be why I love you, Neil."

He interrupted Sam, pointing back to town, "Look over there above Palermo. A double rainbow. If that isn't an omen, I don't know what is."

"Neil, I want you to get your house above the sea."

The rain squalls found them on the terrace, coming down in steel rods. They ran across the terrace and through the ornate rooms to the parking court. The carriage-man had already raised the top and they splashed back to the ship.

The remaining days passed with clear weather across the Atlantic, a flat sea like an inland pond. In the very middle of the crossing, they saw seabirds sailing in circles above the gray waters, fifteen hundred miles from the nearest land. Neil thought of Beethoven's *Calm Seas, Prosperous Voyage,* and wondered if their voyage to Santa Fe would be truly prosperous.

Early on the last morning they went up to the front of ship for the first sight of America, the lighthouse off Cape Cod, blinking on the horizon. It had been three years since either man had been home on the mainland.

"Sam, don't you want to go to Boston for a few days?"

"I'll go up at winter break. Plenty of time for the family."

"You don't talk about your family much. Haven't you missed them?"

"No, not very much. Again, I am not a very good Italian. "

"So you've moved on from your family?"

"In a way, you and Carrie are my family now. Art, Santa Fe, New York, studios would all be foreign to my real family. They would want me to stay in Boston, get a blue-collar job like my brothers, marry Maria Giovanni or Anna Carrozza next door, forget about art. It's better to wait."

"I like being your new family."

"I don't know how you've deserved it, consorting with such a talented Italian man. You don't have the sensual, bristly moustache of Anna Carrozza."

"The train for Chicago leaves at nine, we can make the terminal in plenty of time. Then to St. Louis, Lamy and Santa Fe."

# 6

# Casa Marriner

Louisa Marriner sat at her desk in the former library of Casa Marriner, the compound of adobe buildings and studios that housed the Lionel Monmouth School of Art. It was the high-ceilinged room that her father, Victor Marriner, built to serve as a repository for his ever-growing collection of art books, now transformed into the main office for all the affairs of the school. Louisa held the title of Fiscal Director

The whole of Casa Marriner lay within three acres on the main residential street of Santa Fe, Camino del Monte Sol. Cottonwood trees and rows of Lombardy poplars shaded the buildings from the fierce sun of the Southwest. Victor bought the original property from a Santa Fe family in the Thirties, now greatly expanded from its first simple house. He continually added new structures and wings until his death in 1960, sixteen years ago. Victor loved quoting, with a tongue in cheek, the Victor Hugo dictum that no gentlemen knew exactly how many rooms were in his house.

If he was an impassioned landscapist of New Mexico images, he also nurtured an obsession for constructing adobe buildings. With his own crew of *adoberos*, he built six separate studios connected with long arms of thick-walled houses, reception rooms, storage buildings, covered loggias, pergolas and two separate chapels. The three acres fairly bulged with improvements, encircled by a high wall with two ornamented gates, heavy with roof-tiles and imbedded terracotta plaques. It was an island to itself in the middle of town and even in Victor's time was poorly maintained, vines left unpruned and grassy corners uncut. Victor was happier building anew rather than keeping up what was already there.

Louisa inherited Casa Marriner on Victor's death, sharing the bequest with her brother, Richard. It was, in fact, all that Victor had to pass on to his children. His other assets were but a few dollars in the local bank and a great stack of his own paintings, many unfinished. This was a time when mud residential buildings in Santa Fe were officially appraised with no or little value and unfinished paintings were valued as nothing more than canvas and paint. Louisa and Richard sailed through probate without the burden of death taxes.

Richard had no interest in Santa Fe or Casa Marriner, leaving Louisa to live there and make what income she could out of it. Many years before he had left his hometown to become a writer of academic volumes on the Mount Athos monasteries and Greek mysticism. His books of these subjects became the standard texts in many universities; they gave him a steady, small income from royalties.

Richard was all but a mystic himself, spending months each winter walking from monastery to monastery on the peninsula forbidden to women. He wrote at his house on the island of Patmos, seldom visiting his sister, although communicating regularly with long letters. His absence from Santa Fe did not evidence a lack of love for his sister. He much preferred her visit in his island house to a stay by him in the United States, so when the royalties built up enough he sent her a plane ticket.

Louisa tried renting the studios and houses separately, but the day-to-day management of income property made her worry, gave her a chronic rash. When Lionel Monmouth approached her about leasing the entire property for his new graduate school of art, she readily agreed. As part of the deal, Lionel hired her as his assistant and allowed her to stay on in Victor's own house. Lionel's staff looked after repairs and other maintenance, allowing Louisa's rash to disappear. It was a most agreeable arrangement for both parties.

She said "Enter" to Lionel's knock.

"Ah, my dear, this is the day. Our new faculty arriving on the hour," he said. Lionel was tall and thin, his prematurely gray hair assiduously clipped into a Vandyke mustache and beard. What he lacked in body weight he made up for in the sheer abundance of his hair. His inherent awkwardness of movement was emphasized by his height; swinging a long arm out to make a point in his lectures he often banged his knuckles on the blackboard or with an earnest wave, he could accidentally sweep all his books off of the desk onto the floor. His students learned to write down whatever it was that those gestures endorsed.

"Lionel, your family has come through for you, once again."

"Margaret did wonders. The two young men seem highly qualified with their Summa Cum Laude degrees, even if Neil is my nephew. I don't want a hint of nepotism. Miss Ferrand seems to have just barely graduated, according to the letters I got from her tutors. I am worried about her capability; she wants to teach art history and the women's role in the arts, more than the practical classes. Perhaps she can't do much damage there."

"You mustn't be such a misogynist. I am sure she will fit in. We need another woman on the faculty, a younger woman. Gloria is barely a teacher at all, just babbling about her own genius and how no museum gives her the respect due."

"She may babble, but she inspires the women students, especially. She is a true modernist and the students see that, absorb her message."

Gloria Gallentine had been with the Monmouth School from the start, taking no salary at all the first year. For the two decades before, she was a highly visible and vocal member of Santa Fe's Modernist group of painters. She owned her own house and studio on Upper Canyon Road, paid for solely with the proceeds of her art. Her prodigious output could not be absorbed by the few local collectors of Modernism, so the canvases built up in stacks against her studio and gallery walls. She was an inspiration on a personal level as well, openly discussing with anyone who would listen her preference for women.

Lesbianism in Santa Fe was not necessarily a detriment to personal and social success. The older Hispanic community, while not actually approving of women living together, did nothing to make them feel unwelcome. By and large, the many women who sought refuge in Santa Fe came there with more money, ability and East Coast Establishment connections than anyone else in the existing Anglo community. It was an invasion not unlike the Normans taking over England, until mannish women owned many of the biggest houses on the East Side of town.

Louisa said, "Lionel, I was worried about having so much on deposit with our local bank. I've converted most of it to Treasury notes and bills. Although the total is impressive, it will all have gone out by spring. Salaries, the new housing expenses, studio facilities that need upgrading and the general maintenance of the place will siphon every bit off by this time next year."

"But that is not bad, is it?"

"No, indeed. If we can keep this momentum going for the next year, we will see an actual profit. We just need to get through this year and have as good press coverage again. No added expenses, though."

"How times change. Think about our paltry condition a few years ago. Who would have thought you had such a way with money, Louisa?"

"It is curious. I love doing it, making accounts balance. Actually looking after the property made me edgy, but this is so different. More abstract, I think."

"I consider myself a fortunate man because of you."

"Myself, as well, Lionel."

# 7

# Osmotic Elation

When Neil and Sam arrived at the train station in Lamy, Fortuno, a stout man in his sixties and the school's driver, met them with the old station wagon that still passed for the official school vehicle. After packing their cases into the rear of the wagon, he settled so deep into the drivers seat that his view was through the top of the steering wheel. He drove the fifteen miles to town with an impressive slowness, ignoring cars that raced to pass or such newly installed impediments as stop signs.

"Mister Monmouth is happy you have come."

"How are things going, Fortuno?" Neil said.

"Many workman to get things ready. All the studios need painting and the women are cleaning all the small buildings. We have many new students soon."

"Do you remember me about ten years ago? Here for the summer?"

"You were not a happy boy, I remember."

"That's true. Maybe I'll be happier now."

It had been a wet summer and the drive to Santa Fe was through green grass and wildflowers. Neil remembered his summer in Santa Fe as very dry, no rain until the very end. Despite the heat of the days back then, the nights were cool enough for a blanket. They drove up hill through the junipers and pinons of Old Santa Fe trail to the main gate. Fortuno delivered them outside the entrance to the main house at the compound. Lionel heard the car on the gravel drive and waited on the front portal for them.

"My dear nephew, welcome. And you are Sam Bonifacio, I am sure. First in your class. Most impressive."

Neil said, "We're glad to be here, Lionel. Fourteen days since we left Gordes."

"Fortuno, please take the men's trunks to the Roman Studio." He returned to the loaded car and drove around the end of the house.

"Roman Studio?" Neil asked. "I don't remember which one that is."

"Our very best. Victor built it in nineteen forty-eight, I believe, after an Italian sojourn. You've never seen so much crown molding washed with burnt sienna outside Italy, and the walls are thick enough that the closets live totally within them. You must, alas, share the smallish bedroom, but the studio itself is sixty feet long, ample for both of you at your personal work, I would imagine. There's a perfunctory kitchen, as well, for the nights that the dining hall is closed."

"It sounds perfect, Mister Monmouth," Sam said.

"Come in. We have iced tea waiting and I can hear the details of your trip. Then I can show you and Sam around the school buildings. I am sure, Neil, you will remember some of it from your last summer visit. Was that eight or nine years ago?"

"Ten, I think."

"So you were fifteen, then."

"Fortuno said I was unhappy, but I have fond memories."

"Fifteen-year-old boys often look more unhappy than they really are. They have much to consider, the vista of life yet to come."

The three of them sat down in Lionel's office, the former sitting room next to Louisa's library. After pouring out the glasses, Lionel sat down with the two men.

"Louisa tells me that the finances of Monmouth School have never been better. But I do have some concerns," he said.

"Are you worried about us?" Neil asked.

"Not at all. What troubles me is the fragile nature of our little school, buffeted by so much publicity from *The New York Times*, and now other sources as well. A television news team just left here a couple of weeks ago. Even French television has sent an inquiry."

"Are you afraid of getting too large, then?"

"It could ring a death knell for the intimate nature of our teaching. The wisdom we imparted to two or three students in a seminar of many hours may not be possible when we have fifteen students, or twenty-five."

Sam said, "It's still very small by European standards, though. There is a famous class in Art History at the Beaux Arts that often has five hundred students."

"I know," Lionel said, "but they aren't the ones who swept to success in New York. Miss Noggidge and Mr. Basse-Noir gained their notable talents by osmotic elation here, by being immersed in our heady maelstrom of ideas about art, its production, and the goals and aesthetics of art. This was enough to elevate them above their fellows."

"What, exactly, did you teach them here?"

"I read them many first hand accounts of artistic matters. Matisse's, Van Gogh's, Cezanne's, who wrote a great deal about his artistic intentions, and Rilke's, who wrote about what Cezanne wrote. Ruskin had odd ideas that make students think, gets them arguing. Turner wrote about technique and direction. There are many more. Even Chinese writers were concerned with art. I've unearthed a few Latin and Greek thinkers who thought and wrote about art."

"And that was enough, just sitting down and talking about art?"

"That is perhaps a simplification of the process, but apparently that is what is lacking elsewhere. There, students get plenty of practical advice and drawing lessons, but little in the way of inspired direction. And whatever that is could be in danger of getting submerged in sheer numbers. It may be possible only in the small tutorial."

Neil said, "We'll do our best."

"Indeed. For now, I ask the two of you to concentrate on the excellence of your concrete instruction. We've lacked that until now, the teaching of technique in depth. *Plein air* for you, and Studio Techniques for you, Sam. I will continue with the seminars. Let me show you around the marvels of Casa Marriner."

"No, uncle, I think we'll unpack now. We'll do the full tour another time, if you don't mind."

"Don't forget the faculty dinner tonight. Here at my house at seven. Very casual so don't worry about what to wear."

The two men finished their iced tea and followed Lionel's directions to their new quarters.

# 8

# Poison Cookies

Their studio was on the far edge of the Marriner compound, actually abutting the perimeter wall. A small enclosed garden served as the entry, across which the large doors with peeling sienna paint stood open, thanks to Fortuno. Victor Marriner delighted to tell his friends that a man with a top hat on horseback could ride at top speed through those doors, a Junoesque woman with him on the saddle.

Sam and Neil walked into the studio, a grand room with sixteen foot ceilings, two stone fireplaces, large square beams carved with Latin dictums and a north studio window across the whole end wall. *Labor Omnia Vincit. In Vino Veritas. Ad Astra Per Asperum. Ars Longa, Vita Brevis.* were repeated in succession on the sides of the beams. Surely, a cardinal of middle rank would feel at home at the refectory table in the middle of the room, issuing edicts for the Promulgation of the Faith.

The small bedroom, bath and kitchen led off the end opposite the window. Fortuno had taken their bags to the bedroom, but left their easel packs in the studio.

"When Lionel said housing will be provided, he really meant it," Neil said.

"It beats the socks off the Café Metropole."

The bedroom had a pair of twin beds with headboards painted as griffins; Lionel was correct about the closet being contained completely within the end wall. The bathroom was off to the side. If it was small, the bath-tub appeared to be of English manufacture, Neil thought, longer than a tall man and deep enough to float free above the bottom. What passed for a kitchen was built into the sides of the hallway giving access to the bedroom.

They unpacked their clothes and books, and put away their toiletries in the bathroom

Neil said, "I think we could learn to love it here."

In a corner of the studio were two carved, hardwood easels, each capable of holding a canvas eight foot square. Neil rolled one of them over to the studio window with north light, pulled over a side table and unpacked his canvas bag of paints, brushes and palette knives. He unstrapped one of the unfinished waterside scenes that he had started in Cabasson and placed it, lonely and small, on the huge easel.

"Sam, there's room for both easels, back-to-back, beside this window."

"I'm going to take the other end of the studio and I don't think I'll need an easel for a while. I have a mind to paint on an unstretched piece of canvas, flat on the floor. I've been thinking a lot about how to do a series that way."

At that moment the brass bell next to the still open front doors rang and a short, stocky man strode in, carrying a plate covered with aluminum foil. He wore black trousers and a black turtle neck, and Neil thought he must surely dye his hair, an unnatural shade of light copper.

"Hello, I'm Randolph Eisenhart, also on the faculty here. My wife, Bella, has baked some cookies here for you, despite my protestations. We live in the house across the way. Do you like cookies?"

"Please tell your Bella thanks so much. I'm Neil and he's Sam."

"You're getting settled, then?"

"We're almost done. Two suitcases and two back packs disappear quickly in this studio."

Eisenhart looked up at the ceiling and around the studio. "It certainly pays to be the nephew of the headmaster. I have wanted this studio for years, but your Uncle Lionel thinks I deserve a much smaller one, without north light."

Neil assessed this early, totally unprovoked attack and decided to ignore it. "I feel very lucky to have it."

"I doubt luck entered the equation at all."

Sam said, "You get right to the point, don't you?"

"It makes things easier. At least I haven't been ousted from my field of teaching as well."

"And what is that?"

"Problems of the Large Painting. All of the students want to paint large canvases because it's what they think New York wants. Few, very few, know how to do it. I struggle to show them, with some small break-throughs now and then. Mine has always been the most popular class at the school."

"So Noggidge and Basse-Noire were your students?"

"They gave me not a word of credit at all, only your Lionel and the school."

Neil said, "I am sure it wasn't on purpose. Lionel is not petty."

"At least, to family he's not. I'll see you again at the faculty dinner, tonight. I am sure we will hear about what new honors will be lavished on you boys."

Sam said, "We can't wait."

Eisenhart left the studio and the two men looked at one another.

Sam said, "That went well, didn't it?"

Neil said, "I hope the rest of the faculty aren't as sweet as he is. He has a pile of chips on his shoulder. I wonder why?"

"He's a jerk. An ass-hole. Some people just come that way."

"There's more to the story. I don't think Lionel, who hates discord, would have consciously discriminated against anybody. "

"He didn't. Eisenhart looks for injustice, collects it, whether it exists or not. He's the type you need to stand up to. He only understands someone who fights him back, steps on his neck."

"I can't think why he came over here at all, if he already hates us so. He doesn't even know us. I wonder if the cookies are safe to eat, a little poison added after mama baked them."

Sam said, "He came here to size us up as adversaries, and also, it's no fun to hate if you can't see its affects."

"I want to get his bad aura out of our studio." He opened the casements in the studio window, as if fresh air would flush out Eisenhart's presence.

"Better summon up your grandmother."

"Sam, I don't know how you feel about it right now, but at the outset, despite Eisenhart, everything feels right here."

"We'll see."

"The Marriner compound has magic everywhere, especially in our Roman studio. Don't you feel them, the years of painting and the long nights of talk about painting? The woodwork has absorbed them like wax and linseed oil."

"We'll see."

Neil returned to his easel. He looked at the drips of paint on the dark hardwood and the encrusted archipelagos of color on the bottom bracket. Was this one of Victor Marriner's own easels? How many hours of work did this represent? A lifetime, Neil supposed, probably a happy lifetime. He made a note to look for examples of Victor's work, perhaps at the museum downtown, to make a connection between the contentment he saw here with an actual canvas.

# 9

# Pretty Little Grasses

Lionel pulled together the liquor and wine bottles, glasses, limes and lemons, napkins and bar towel needed for the drinks that he would serve to his guests. The liquors available at his bar were generic and often in the large bottles with handles. He served drinks in the glasses that the French sold for jellies and conserves. Lionel had a keen sense of academic parsimony, avoiding ostentation or profligacy: no Oxford don in rooms with linen-fold paneling, sideboards heavy with Georgian silver.

His cook, Rita, handled the rest of the night's dinner, set the table, cooked and served the food. These were at least monthly occasions during the school year, a gathering of faculty, their wives or lovers and occasional guests. It was an important tradition for keeping alive a spirit in the school. Lionel hoped, with his faculty evenings, to create a Japanese-like consensus, everybody pulling the same direction.

He always spoke after the dinner, a short speech outlining the "state of the school." Lionel was an expert in his own setting, painstakingly choosing the food, the wine, the number of candles on the table and where each guest must sit. The food was uniformly good, but not lavish or abundant. A roast sometimes, fried fish and rice quite often, enchiladas on lesser occasions. Wine was from country jugs, decanted to locally thrown stoneware pitchers, already on the table. The wine-glasses themselves were heavy glass, the green cast disclosing their recycled origin. Tonight there were only eight at the table which could seat many more.

Lionel inspected the table that Rita had set. He approved its festive air, without pretension or guile. There were mismatched sterling silver forks and knives, all English and well-polished, white French porcelain plates from which most of the gold rim had been worn, and honest cotton napkins, ironed and starched.

"Rita, are there more candles for the side board?" This was Lionel's one indulgence in an otherwise hospitable but simple dinner.

"That's all of them, Lionel. I'll get more this week."

"It always looks better with more of them."

"Yes. I'll see to it."

Rita had worked for Victor Marriner before Lionel. She liked Lionel, understood his insistence upon simple, almost Quaker ways, but she worshipped the memory of Victor. In the golden receptacle of memory, Victor's choices and manners verged upon godlike. There was in some of the older Hispanics in Santa Fe a delight and respect for outrageous behavior, if it came from the "El Patron." Egalitarian, simple good manners were neither expected nor appreciated, a New England plant that did not transplant well.

Where the current dinner verged on the penurious, Victor's would have had an éclat and style impossible for Lionel to recreate. Game, out-of-season vegetables, French wines, English cheeses and sweet soufflés for dessert. Early on, Lionel asked her how Victor would have wanted something done and the answer invariably displeased him. Victor ran his life like he painted, and he built Casa Marriner with gusto and little regard for expense. So now Lionel and Rita had come to an understanding for, if not an admiration of, what he called "the frayed white collar."

Louisa Marriner came early to the dinner. Her long face and dark eyes recalled a Byzantine icon without its golden nimbus, her dress perfectly matched that spirit with heavy folds of dark maroon, as if run up from castle draperies. Her only jewelry was a golden crucifix with garnets that hung almost to her waist.

She said, "The young lady, Carrie Ferrand, arrived and I showed her the quarters we decided upon for her. She was thrilled with the casita. She has very good manners and, I must say, I think the calm presence that denotes a good teacher."

"Splendid. Did you ask her for tonight?"

"Yes. She may be late."

"Was she not on the train?"

"No, she drove herself here from New York. Admirable spirit."

The other guests started to arrive. Gloria Gallentine wore slacks and military jacket of matching black; no jewelry or makeup. Randolph and Bella Eisenhart were next. Bella was a short, pretty woman whose obvious love of good food and drink had started to show. Perhaps there were other, more personal motives for her neighborly baking. Trafford Norwell, the last of the existing faculty arrived on his own, wearing a sports jacket and a black tie.

Louisa greeted him warmly with a hug. "Trafford, I think you'll be delighted with the three new, young additions to our faculty. I've only met Carrie Ferrand, who will fit in admirably." Louisa had already started a campaign to have Carrie accepted, worried that Lionel's questioning would spread.

Neil and Sam arrived, wearing their travel-wrinkled best. Lionel introduced them to the others and let them circulate on their own. When Carrie arrived, he took her personally around, gave introductions and stayed on to see how she fit in. She wore a simple black long dress with her blonde hair up, held with a tortoise-shell comb.

Soon the noise of the conversations accelerated and the guests moved slowly from grouping to grouping. Lionel observed with approval that his congregation was getting along well, no discernible discord. He was an able host, replenishing drinks before they were empty.

After an hour, Rita announced that dinner was ready. Lionel seated Louisa to his right and Carrie to his left. He put Sam at the far end, with the other two women at each side. The other men filled the centers on each side, Neil next to Trafford. Rita passed the platters with food to each of the guests and they poured their wine from the pitchers themselves. The dinner was under way.

Gloria Gallentine turned to Neil, sitting beside her, and said, "Mister Bronson, I know your mother, Margaret. We went to school together, ever so long ago. She was a force to be dealt with even then, a young Minerva breaking the hearts of all the immortals of both genders."

"Even if I'm not broken hearted, I think she's divine, too. Please call me Neil."

"You're our new *plein air* instructor. So very quaint. I really thought that went out in the last century when we stopped studying how angels ought to fly and grinding the perfect blue color for Madonna's shawl. I can't think why Lionel included it in the curriculum, modern art is the bellwether here."

"Partly, because I asked him to. I spent the summer in France painting outside, and I came to believe it has value for any young artist."

"A total waste of time, learning about purple horizons, wisps of pinkish clouds and foregrounds with pretty little grasses and wildflowers. True art is about ideas and how color and form can describe them"

"The best landscapes are concerned with those same ideas, color and form, as well. I think that the young eye can associate with those when they can actually see them, rather than mere talk in the classroom about them."

"The best art of today is concerned only with ideas, not scenes or the depiction of objects. New ideas, stunning ideas."

"So ideas cannot exist in a landscape?"

"You're a nice young man. We'll just have to disagree." With that she cut off the conversation and turned to Sam on her other side.

Neil turned to Trafford Norwell at his left and introduced himself.

Norwell said, "I couldn't help hearing Gloria expound, but take solace in the fact that you're not alone. She thinks my classes in Still Life date even further back from the Sixteenth Century, so you're at last three centuries more modern. Gloria can be a pain in the ass."

Gloria leaned across Neil and said, "I heard that, Norwell. There are many enemies of Modern Art lurking here."

Neil turned back to Norwell. "It is amusing, since in undergraduate art school and in London graduate school, non-objective and color field art was what we were taught. I thought that was all there was. I had to come onto *plein air* landscape work on my own, with long visits to London's museums and then actually doing it in France. I did it all with Sam, at the table's end."

"What you find on your own is always the best."

"Is that how you found your specialty?"

"Absolutely. When I was at art school, social significance was all in the air. Instructors insisted upon it. Political matters were an acceptable substitute, but painting for its own sake was vilified. My professors insisted that art must have a message. I gave in to that on my master's thesis and painted sleeping drunks on San Francisco streets with well-dressed matrons looking down from upper floor windows, heavy draperies pulled back."

"How do you feel about that now?"

"I believe a painting is not the platform for political comment."

Neil said, "*Guernica* is what professors still talk about."

"Startling as it was, it did nothing to stop the war or future wars. Picasso painted twenty thousand other paintings that weren't political. "

"So art professors are evil?"

"Some are, like Gloria over there." He waited for a response from Gloria, but she was busy lecturing Sam. He continued, "Maybe next week, you, Sam and Carrie can come to my house for dinner. I'm a good cook and I would like for you to meet my partner. Say Thursday or Friday, let me know."

"We'd like that."

At the other side of the table, Carrie talked to Lionel.

She said, "Mister Monmouth, tell me about your classes. How do you organize them?"

"I confess to being vastly disorganized. We have a room in the main building with a large table and twelve or thirteen comfortable chairs with cushions. I try to arrive early, with a pile of books, and sit at the middle seat of the table. Then I just read passages aloud and ask for comments. Each class is different. Sometimes I'll press the French writers, sometimes the Chinese."

"It sounds like heaven. I wish London had had a course like that."

"The title of the course may be pretentious, but I continue it anyway: Aesthetic Considerations. Mostly, we talk about What is Art and Who is the Artist. It is amazing how the time passes. I prepare a long reading list, some of which they do read."

"So, I can't resist. What is Art?"

"Ah, you won't trap me there. I'll arrange an extra seat for you at the table, maybe a hard-backed chair for the curious."

Louisa, who sat across from Carrie, said, "Lionel has a favorite quotation about art, which he is holding back: *Art is nature to advantage dressed.* It's from Alexander Pope."

Lionel said, "But in the seminar, that is just where the gate opens. We find other avenues for art without bringing it down to the lowest denominator. I detest those who say every common action is an art, like cooking or gardening.

We have spirited days on that matter."

The dinner conversation continued at high pitch, between changing twos and threes around the table. Neil made a point of not looking toward Eisenhart, who spent most of the meal talking to Carrie, with many affectionate pats of her hand. Gloria Gallentine had nothing more to say to Neil and answered his questions monosyllabically. Lionel ended the evening with a very short speech, welcoming the newcomers. He said there were forty new students, selected from several hundred who eventually applied. Seven former students were returning. It would be the faculty's goal to burnish them all and send them on. This would be a pivotal year for their small school.

# 10

# Matriculando

A light snow fell that September night before the students were to arrive, covering the mountains with white and leaving several inches on the Camino del Monte Sol section of town. The clouds had passed and it was bright sun and ankle-deep slush for this first day.

Neil came to the main building early to read the catalog of courses drawn up by Lionel. On the third page was his entry:

*Plein air Landscape Painting: Three times a week, MWF, TTS, mornings at 9. Three credits. Techniques of painting landscapes out-of-doors, field trips to nearby locations. Portable easel, paints, brushes, solvents available as "Kit No. 2", local art supply stores. $450.00, required. Mr. Bronson.*

And there was another course:

*Theory of Landscape Painting: Twice a week, TT, afternoons at 2. Two credits. Lectures and discussions of current and past landscape work. No text or supplies required. Mr. Bronson.*

The lecture course was a surprise for Neil. Lionel had not mentioned it in his letters or discussions. Neil wondered just how he would put this together in the few days left before classes actually began. The crush of students and faculty in the main building all worked on the signing up process, so this was not a time for discussion with Lionel. It would have to wait until afternoon.

Of course, the salary for the year of work was generous, but Neil had not anticipated a lecture course. He somehow thought they would all be courses taught in the field, practical experience courses. How would he be at a lecture?

He thumbed through the rest of the catalogue. Carrie would teach two courses, Work on Paper and Problems of the Small Painting. Neil knew she would be good at both of these. Sam had, as Lionel had agreed to, all the Studio Techniques workshops. He just started to read the entries for Randolph Eisenhart's courses, when the man himself walked up.

"Good morning, Bronson. It will be interesting to see how many students sign up for your *plein air* field trips. I would say very few, just off the top of my head. My experience tells me that students today want to know the way to edgy, difficult work. Work that will resound in New York."

"You are right, of course. I'll be happy to get ten or twelve."

"Yes, indeed."

"By noon, we'll know. What will you do if all forty new students want your class?" Neil asked.

"I'll divide them into two classes. Twenty is enough for a full ship."

That was nearly what happened when the counting was finished at noon. Neil had eighteen students, which he divided into two classes, MWF and TTS. Eisenhart garnered thirty eight students, which he also divided. Carrie's offerings were accepted by mostly woman students. Gloria Gallentine, like Eisenhart, appealed to all the new students and her classes were jammed full. Norwell's courses were much like Neil's, in that a total of twenty signed up for his two Still Life and single Portrait classes. Realism and objective painting was not to be a strong point at the Monmouth School this year.

Lionel's seminars in Aesthetics were the only required courses, so he assigned them into small groups to meet throughout the week.

As the matriculation gathering came to a close, Carrie came over to Neil.

She said, "It's been such a rush since we got here. I've barely said hello. Do you have time to talk?"

"Yes, right now."

"Let's go for a walk," she said. The went out to the main gate and walked the Camino towards town.

"I've missed seeing you."

Neil said, "Me, too. It's been several weeks. Did you stay on at Gordes for long?"

"I stayed a week with Nicole."

"What's she going to do now? She will miss you."

"I know. She told me so. She may come here for a visit this winter. That's a very slow season at the Auberge."

"Nicole is strongly attracted to you. Both Sam and I noticed."

"She's just a friend, Neil. No love interest at all."

"That isn't what she would say."

"But it *is* what I would say."

"Okay."

Carrie took Neil by the arm and said, "Let's sit here for a while."

They sat on a low adobe wall in front of an adjoining property. Snow from the night before had mostly melted, leaving rivulets of runoff along the Camino and dripping trees. The mountains in the distance sported a saddle of white, foretelling an early winter in Santa Fe.

"Last night at the faculty dinner Sam asked me to marry him."

"He said nothing to me about it. But, it's not a surprise, really. Sam has loved you for a long time."

"I didn't know what to tell him."

"How about yes?"

"He's not the one I love."

Neil thought better than to pursue that line of conversation. "So what did you tell him?"

"I asked him to give me some time. A couple of months."

"Wise. I can see you and Sam married, though. It would keep the two I love most together in my life."

"I was worried how you would feel about losing Sam."

"Would I be losing him?"

"Probably not. You will always be in both our lives. A marriage is strange way to validate what the three of us have."

"I agree. So you're not deciding right now?"

"No. Down deep, Neil, I had hoped it was you who had asked me and I would be having this conversation with Sam, instead."

"But you wouldn't be having this conversation because you would have accepted me. Isn't that right?"

"I confess, yes."

"Carrie, I love you. But our marriage would not work out. Your marriage to Sam might just work. He adores you, and that makes up for a lot."

"I suppose. Why can't there be marriages between three people? Why do you just have to choose only one, when your heart says two?"

"I like the idea. Please say hello to Mister, Missus and Mister Bronson, they're spouses, you know."

"You make fun, but it might work better than anything else."

"Or better yet, we'd take your last name. The Misters and Missus Ferrand. Wouldn't your father be pleased?"

"Let's drop it, Neil." She jumped off the wall and took Neil's hand. They headed back to the Casa Marriner in silence.

As they walked through the gates, she said, "I forgot to tell you. Your exhibit with at Hetty's gallery is for one week only and it's opening on December seventh. I thought the timing would amuse you."

"Couldn't be more appropriate. The sinking of more Americans."

"I don't think it will be a sinking. After some initial questions, she was quite excited about it. When the crates arrived, she called me, and she loves the paintings. Especially yours. She is sure it will be a sell-out."

"Wouldn't that be nice? I don't expect we can go over for opening night, though."

"No. She'll send me a proof of the invitation when its ready."

"Thanks for arranging it all. I understand your constant love and concern, and wish there was some way to reciprocate it."

"There's a very easy way."

"Other than that, I mean."

Neil kissed Carrie lightly on the mouth and held her for a while. She smiled at him in return. He walked across the parking court toward his studio.

The rest of matriculation day at the Monmouth School, the students and the teachers were asked to mingle and meet each other. There were groups of conversing students on the walls and benches all around the main buildings and studios. Neil could hear the excitement in their voices, the hope and innocence.

At the studio, Neil felt a need for a nap. He slept for a hour in the bedroom and woke to the sound of Sam in the studio room. He got up and stood at the studio door. Sam had spread a large square of canvas on the floor and was painting long stripes of pale gray from side to side.

"You can't start too soon." Sam said, seeing Neil.

"Good for you. I crashed in the other room."

"This altitude takes the wind out of your sails."

"It does me, for sure. Sam, do you have something to tell me?"

"Oh, she told you," he replied with a smile.

"This morning."

"I saw her at dinner and she looked so beautiful. I knew I better start asking her now, since she's going to take a long time to make up her mind."

"That doesn't bother you?"

"Sure it bothers me."

"I told Carrie that your marriage would keep the two people I love most together in my life."

"You're worrying that we'll leave you all alone."

"I always worry."

# 11

# A Line of Dark Umber

Neil's first Tuesday class was scheduled in two days, almost before he had time to think about how it would all work. He arranged with Fortuno Furth to drive the Monmouth School bus, a recycled thirty seater that Lionel bought from the local school system, out to the Galisteo River with nine students and their equipage. It would take twenty-five minutes to get there, so the first field trip would be only two hours.

All nine students were aboard when Neil arrived with his easel and pack in the parking court. They had reserved a spot for him in the seat next to Fortuno. He wished them all good morning and they were off.

Salazar Ortega sat behind him. He introduced himself and said, "Mister Bronson, I hope you won't mind, but may I ask you a question?"

"Certainly."

"You look so young. Ollie and I were wondering how old you are."

"I'm twenty-five."

"When we saw you in the parking court, I said you couldn't be more than twenty. Ollie wondered if we're going to get our money's worth out of a teacher so young."

"Who knows, Salazar. Maybe not."

"It was a joke, but it sort of scares me that someone so young could know enough to teach others."

"It's good to run scared. And how old are you?"

Salazar said, "I'm twenty-five, too. Ollie's twenty."

"Maybe I'm young for a teacher and you're old for a student."

Neil thought he might stop this before it went any further. It was a good time to start a description of what they could expect from his classes. He told them that they would go out each day, weather permitting, and set their easels up in one location. Everybody would paint the same scene, teacher included, for about two or so hours. Neil would paint a demonstration for them to start the class. Then he would look at each of their paintings with comments and suggestions.

When they arrived at the Galisteo River, there was a slow stream of water in the stream bed. The term "river" might have been more of a hope than a reality. Years ago, Lionel brought Margaret and Neil out to Galisteo for a summer picnic. What Neil knew they would see there, what they would paint, were the intense colors of the escarpment and the adjoining grasses and shrubbery. The escarpment itself was an album of earth reds and burnt siennas, thirty feet high and undulating along the side of the stream bed. Clusters of dark green pinons and orange-green junipers came right up to the stream, with stretches of gray sagebrush and chamisa.

He led the class a few hundred feet from where Fortuno parked the bus and set up his easel with the canvas turned away from the sun. If the students worried about his young age, his Provencal straw farm-hat had the authority of a summer outside at the easel, the brim bent up in the right places. He spread the paints and brushes on a small shelf below the canvas and asked them to gather around while he started.

His first line on the canvas was of bright cadmium red, near the top to denote the horizon. He painted several more lines to indicate the hills below the horizon, then a bold earth red sweep across the canvas for the escarpment. A few quick squiggles below that described the sagebrush to come. In five minutes, he had the major elements of the scene blocked in without details.

He said as he painted, "It's better, I think, to try to paint only a small portion of what you see. The whole view can confuse. So all of you get started and paint in a horizon first, then the major thing you see. Smaller details after that. Don't worry about color in this first sketch. Use reds and siennas to outline things."

The students spread around and set up their easels in a large semi-circle behind Neil's easel. As the class got under way Neil went from student to student with advice, sometimes taking the brush from the student to make a point. He had a list of the students provided by Lionel and identified each with a name. When they all were at work, he went back to his own easel. After an hour of leaving them on their own, he started another round of the semi-circle.

He walked up to Ollie Bainbridge, obviously a farm boy from his sturdy frame. He reminded Neil of a younger Sam with his dark hair and solid stance. He also had Sam's bearing at the easel, a posture that claimed art was serious business .

"Ollie, you've made a good start with a large scene. Next time, though, I would focus down your canvas, paint a smaller scene. Later you can do the grand version. It's easier to look at a smaller collection of objects, letting the small scene represent the larger one. Where are you from, Ollie?"

"Kansas, Mister Bronson. I was raised on a farm. Three brothers, but I'm the only one that went to university."

"So you want to be a painter?"

"Maybe an art teacher or a commercial artist."

"What do your brothers think of that?

"Not much."

"They'll be proud of you eventually. May take time, though."

"I'll let you tell them that. In Kansas, art is not a proper field for men."

"And that's why Kansas is in the middle of nowhere and stays there."

Ollie smiled and turned back to his easel. How difficult it was to find your heart's desire, even without the opprobrium of a provincial family, Neil thought. He looked at Ollie's large hands and thought it would be a brave soul who told him that he was not a man.

He moved on to Segunda Plaith, a nineteen year old from New York City. She told Neil that her mother saw *The New York Times* piece and insisted she come to Santa Fe. Mother was hard to say no to, she said.

Neil said, "How do you like Santa Fe so far?"

"I hate it. I like the city."

"It won't be long and we're both back in New York."

"So you hate it, too?"

"No, but, like you, I came here to please my family. You have to be very strong to resist family."

Her version of the scene had dark lines around every object in the landscape, as if she preferred the grade school coloring book. Her picture had an appealing, childlike quality, the shapes of the landscape converted to simple cut-outs with dark perimeters. Neil thought of the Misery paintings. She had seen a sadness in this scene that eluded Neil.

"I see what you've done here, Segunda. It reminds me of a Rouault with those black lines."

"To me it asks to have lines around everything. It makes it look neater and not so wild."

"Good work. Keep it up."

The red-headed, brown-eyed Salazar Ortega was next. He stood a few inches taller than Neil, with broad shoulders and long-fingered hands. He had painted in great detail the bottom portion of the canvas with nothing on the upper two-thirds, not even a sketch of what would come. Several of the sagebrushes he had wiped out and repainted several times. He was working on the leaves of a small willow in the foreground with painstaking strokes.

"So what has happened to the top of your painting, Salazar?"

"I'll get to it in time. I have to completely finish the first things before moving on."

"When you're eating dinner, do you finish all your potatoes first, then move on to all the peas, and then the meat?"

The light, humorous touch did not seem to work. Salazar looked at him with an angry face. "Yes. Is there something wrong with that?"

"There's nothing wrong with your way. But probably it's not a good plan of attack for painting. When you do finally get to the top half, you might not remember what you had in mind for it. You might try harder to paint all parts of the canvas at the same time. "

"I like it this way."

"We'll see how it turns out for you. So, tell me, Salazar, why are you twenty-five years old and just now starting a graduate course in art? What have you been doing for the last few years?"

"I've been in the Army."

"How was it in the Army?"

"I liked the service. I enlisted and spent four years in Germany."

"Why did you leave?"

"My father wanted me to come home to Santa Fe. He said he needed me. The tuition for this school was his lure to get me home."

Neil thought Salazar had none of the qualities he associated with a dutiful son. "You're family lives here?"

"I was born here, Mister Bronson."

"Somehow, Mister Bronson doesn't seem right, considering our ages. Maybe you should just call me Neil."

"Won't that confuse the other students?"

"Perhaps. So call me Neil in private and Mister Bronson in front of the others."

"I'll like that." Salazar's anger dissolved.

The field trip passed quickly for Neil. As departure time approached, he showed the students his finished painting. It required still a few deft touches in the solitude of the studio, which Neil pointed out. A thin line of dark, reddish umber along the top of the escarpment would emphasize the sharpness of the cliff edge. It would be easier to insert that when the other paints were dry. A similar thin line along the horizon, this one to be a white suffused with violet to break the line between earth and sky, to bring them together. Some of the shadows needed reworking, which he denoted with the end of his brush.

Ollie asked, "Is it all right in a *plein air* painting to work on it back at the studio?"

"If painting is a life process, does it really matter? The great value of *plein air* is that you can actually see a color or form when you need to see it. Most people cannot remember the subtle changes of hue in the midground. So, in answer to your question, Ollie, I think you should reserve only a very few touches for the studio. Get as much done as you can out here, where you can really see."

Fortuno Furth had them back at Casa Marriner at two minutes before noon. Neil felt the first class had been a success. He was not sure exactly how to get the students to do things his way, learning the reasons he painted that way, before moving on to experiments of their own, patterns different from his own. He would continue, he decided, to teach the class the same way until some other method appeared. It was all he knew how to do.

Sam had been working all morning on his un-stretched canvas, since his first Studio Techniques workshop began just after noon. Neil noted that he had made many changes to the design of the day before. The long gray stripes were interspersed with thinner stripes of slightly darker colors, and between those more even small stripes, darker yet. Behind this curtain of stripes, he had inserted a meandering cloud of warm colors, oranges shading to yellows. Sam's escape route to New York was well under way.

# 12

# Easy Grace

After their first day of classes, it was the evening of the dinner at Trafford Norwell's. Carrie would drive them to the party. Sam and Neil walked over to her casita on the opposite side of the compound. Carrie called for them to come in. She was not quite ready. Hers was a thick walled house with small rooms, small windows and a ceiling so low that with his outstretched hand Neil could touch the vigas above his head. They were a dark brown, shiny with varnish and the rough walls were whitewashed.

She had hung their paintings from Gordes together in the sitting room. Neil had given her three more from their time in Cabasson and she had those in a group on the opposite wall. A French wool blanket was draped over the daybed and a large bouquet of autumn wildflowers sat on the table.

Carrie appeared at the bedroom door, dressed in a scarlet version of the dress she wore to the faculty dinner.

"My goddess," Sam said.

"Cool it, Sam, it's going to be a long evening and we're going to be late," she said.

She tore off the top page of a notebook by the phone, the directions to Norwell's northside house. On the way there, she took several wrong turns before they pulled into the bumpy driveway denoted only by a street number on a low sign. The house sat on a ledge above the pinons with a view down to the lights of Santa Fe.

Norwell was already at the door when they walked up. "A trial to find your way, I know, but maybe the green chile stew will be worth it."

"What a location, Trafford. The whole city below us," Neil said.

"We built it ourselves. Six summers ago. Laid the adobe, did all the carpentry, plastered it, too. Harold installed the electrical system. The only contractor we hired was a plumber."

He led them inside. It was a dark house, with walls the deep earth color of raw adobe, strands of straw sticking out here and there from the mud plaster. Brick floors reflected the light from the wood burning in the fireplace. The room was redolent of pinon smoke and the stew cooking in the other room.

Norwell introduced his partner, Harold, and they had drinks for about a half an hour. Then the five of them sat at the round table where Norwell had already placed bowls of stew, glasses of red wine and a sliced, rustic loaf.

Norwell said, "So, Carrie, how was the first day of classes?"

"Well, I was terrified, of course. It felt like being in a sailboat in a high wind for the first time, but things went better than I thought they would. I first showed them slides of the small paintings that I like: Bonnington, O'Keeffe, Dove, and some small Fauvist Matisses.

"Did the students respond?"

"Not at first. I had paints, canvas and an easel ready, so I asked them to start a painting in the manner of the Matisses I had shown them. I chose one of the two men to begin the process. He was very nervous, starting it with a window, lightly outlined in blue. He was nearly afraid to continue. The rest added their touches, one by one, the women more adept at this public display. I filled in here and there. Then we reworked it totally. At each stage I asked questions. The Fauvist colors we added one at a time, discussing them in turn."

Sam asked, "How did it turn out?"

"As you might imagine, it could have been a dog's breakfast. But we ended up with a reasonably creditable work. The class seemed delighted with the result, so we've agreed to keep doing this for the first weeks, taking different artists each session. Mostly, it was a method, a trick, if you will, to get ideas about art in the air. How the small canvas works, a single gesture saying more than a vast array."

Norwell asked about the first teaching day for each of them in turn.

"I have three very different students who caught my eye the first day,"

Neil said. "I did not want to beat them into submitting to my way of painting, but I tried to get into their way. It seemed to work. I do like to get outside."

Norwell said, "Old Victor Marriner was at his best outside. It's a pity he can't teach a class as well, under his French umbrella in a camp chair. Fortuno lugged all his equipment while Victor considered the light and the view. He should have been born into great estates or have become the pope."

Sam told them of his day. During his recital of the students' nervous start in the studio, Neil watched the easy grace with which Norwell showed his affection for Harold. As he passed new portions of stew, he stopped to place his hand on Harold's shoulder, who looked up at him with a smile.

Neil asked, "Harold, what do you do in Santa Fe?"

"I have a shop on Canyon Road. Indian artifacts, pots, baskets and whatever else catches my eye."

"Does it do well for you?"

"In some years, yes. This summer was good, last one not."

"Where do you buy the pieces?

"Trafford and I go out to the reservations. He paints while I do the bartering. It can take several days of just sitting and talking, drinking coffee, Doctor Peppers and whittling sticks down to nothing to make one purchase. Sometimes we don't even talk, just sit and look at the clouds."

"And Trafford paints their portraits?"

"He's my secret weapon. Most Hopi and Zuni hate the camera, definitely the Navajo. After a couple of summers of our visits, they now look forward to his sketches, I think. They trust artists more than photographers. The artist/artisan tradition is strong in most of the pueblos and reservations."

"It sounds like a winning team. I would give away my family pots, too."

Trafford said, "It's not really as mercenary as it sounds. We respect the native culture and their extraordinary ability to distill beauty from the world around them. I am sure that they recognize this. Harold pays them good prices, the best of any trader, even though he eventually sells the pieces for a profit. Sometimes a good profit."

Harold said, "Just this summer a Zuni family gave me three large pots that had been in the family for generations. I promised to find a museum to purchase them and this week, I did. A purchase from an anonymous trust."

Norwell was an accomplished host, involving each of his three guests personally with questions and comments about their new Santa Fe endeavors. For Neil, he suggested some locales for his field trips, different motifs from the Galisteo Basin. He listened to a description of the intransigent Salazar, offering no suggestions. He had definite ideas about Carrie's small painting classes, to which she listened intently. The small work of Manet should be included, as well as those of Jackson Pollock. Before Sam took up the three courses in Studio Techniques, it had been Norwell's fiefdom, so he had much to impart on that subject, how to calm the anxious students. Most were self-conscious about performing in front of the other students, so care was needed to get them started.

Norwell said, "I have to say, I'm very glad the three of you are now at the school and I hope you'll want to stay. Eisenhart and Gloria have not been a joy to work with."

Neil said, "Eisenhart has some ego problems."

"He also has some problems patting the fannies of the woman students," said Carrie

Sam said, "Has he bothered you, as well?"

She said, "I can take care of myself, Sam. It's the students I worry about."

"So he has come on to you?"

She put her hand over on Sam's wrist. "It isn't a problem."

Norwell moved on to the subject of Gallentine. "Gloria believes that not only is she on the right path, but laws should be passed to prevent others from painting at all. She wants to be the all-mighty, high priestess of non-objective art. The only one on-stage."

Carrie said, "I can get along with Gloria. She's just like my mother, a bigot and an egomaniac. It's all based on the feeling, down deep, that maybe they don't matter. They want to matter more than anything, so they bully others into accepting them. And after many years of that, they have fine-tuned that bullying into an art form itself."

Neil said, "Lionel says that the students love her, though."

Norwell said, "Students like firm opinions, I believe. It may be the true role of the teacher. Expound in black and white, and let the student rebel into the gray zones in silence."

Harold said, "So much for Socratic questioning."

Neil asked Norwell more questions about the school. He particularly wanted to know about Louisa Marriner. In response, Norwell said, "I knew Louisa and Richard from many years ago, when Victor was still alive. I came to Santa Fe to paint in the summers, and I met them at one of Victor's opening night receptions. They were the town's bright young things, an impressive brother and sister combination."

"What age were you then?"

"Mid-twenties, I suppose. Louisa, Richard and I were all about the same age. Their father was such a powerful personality, they both stood back in awe of him. He was a benign power, however, but daunting to have as a father. Just being around him left wounds. Richard went away from Santa Fe rather than fighting him, and I think he's happy in Greece."

"Does he ever come back here for a visit?"

"He was here last summer. Louisa and he are very close. I don't think he'll ever come back here to stay, though."

Harold said, "It must be said that Richard also comes back to Santa Fe to see Trafford. They were lovers, before me."

Norwell said, "That's true. Richard and I were together for a few years. It didn't take, however. I did not want to live on Patmos, in the middle of nowhere, and he had too many memories to stay on with me in Santa Fe. He and Victor would have constantly argued."

Neil asked, "So he still lives in Greece?"

"Yes, he has friends on the island. And Louisa goes there at least once a year for a long stay. He wants Harold and me to visit, but we always have somewhere else on the docket. Casa Marriner doesn't interest Richard at all."

"I can understand."

The evening came to an end and the three young instructors considered that Casa Marriner was more complex than it had appeared.

Neil said, "I really like Norwell and Harold. They treat each other well."

Sam said, "Maybe you should find somebody like Harold."

"I did. You."

Carrie drove them back without comment. She thought it was too late, she was too tired to figure out a smart reponse to what that meant.

# 13

# The Off-White Studio

Neil's next field trip to Galisteo was reduced to six students, the others presumably disappointed with what *plein air* promised and requested transfer to other classes. The three students he had spent most of the last class with were still there, Ollie, Segunda and Salazar. He started the class in the same way, a sample canvas while the six students watched. This time he concentrated on a foreground scene, all the details right in front of him. He could hear Gloria Gallentine deriding his "pretty little grasses and baby-blue wildflowers," but he pressed on. He expanded the real dimensions of the foreground to command the whole canvas. The composition had no mid-ground and only a quick, almost symbolic rendition of the escarpment and horizon in the distance .

Salazar painted on the same canvas he started in the first class, working up on the canvas, finishing each layer as he went. Neil watched without comment. Teasing Salazar about eating all his peas together would do no good at this stage. When the painting had worked its way to the top, he could enter in.

Segunda painted another picture with dark lines around all the bushes, pinons and rocks. Neil said to her, "Your style can serve you well and it somehow suits this landscape. Good work." She beamed at the approval.

Ollie followed his advice from the former class, limiting his composition to a cropped version of the same scene. "That's working, Ollie. Bringing up the colors a bit, I think would help. A stronger red here, some violet here and a clear green here." Ollie responded to suggestion easily and completed the changes Neil asked for right while he watched.

After an hour at his own easel, Neil made the circuit to all the other easels, with comments for each. At Salazar's painting, he still had no comment.

Salazar said, "You don't like what I'm doing, do you?"

"I'm waiting to see what it looks like. I told you before that your process could be improved, but I'm willing to give yours a chance."

"So it had better be a knock-out or you're going to come down on me?"

"Exactly."

"Neil, can I ask you something?"

"Of course," Neil replied, wondering what new direction this first-name divergence would take.

"Since we're the same age, we could be friends?"

"I don't see why not."

"I know there is supposed to be a professor versus student distance, but maybe we could get beyond that. I think we're the same in many ways. It would be nice for me to talk about that."

"When did you have in mind?"

"Dinner, maybe."

"Dinner? Well, let me think about that. Instructors probably should not put students in difficult social situations."

"Tomorrow night and it won't be difficult. I could pick you up around seven and we'd go to a place I know."

"I'll let you know, Salazar."

This was a surprise, a new act, thought Neil. He would have to examine the propriety of teachers having dinner with students, even if they were the same age. It was, he thought, more a matter of position of authority versus position of helplessness. Salazar, the ex-infantry soldier, did not seem in jeopardy. It was full of imagined danger and excitement. He would ask Sam what he thought.

As the bus pulled back into the parking court, the other students rushed to get out first. Fortuno left the bus door open when he left. Neil purposely lingered behind and Salazar had, too.

"Salazar, dinner sounds good. Let's do it."

"I'll see you tomorrow."

Now that he was committed, Sam would probably actively disapprove. Just a few nights ago he had suggested that Neil find someone like Harold. Maybe it was better that he did not consult Sam at all. He knew that there would be criticism there.

Instead of returning to his own studio, he headed up to the main building. He walked through the warren of rooms leading to Louisa Marriner's office, the old library. He knocked and Louisa said Enter.

"Hello, Neil. How are your classes going?"

"Well, I think. Several students dropped out after the first class, but the ones that are still there seem to be making progress."

"I saw the paperwork on those changes. Don't be discouraged, however. Even when we had notably fewer students, they scurried around a bit before finding their right place. I am sure is has nothing to do with you."

"Perhaps. But I have an idea for the class. It involves your father's unfinished paintings."

"What about them?"

"Lionel told me you had a collection of Victor's incomplete paintings here at his studio. Next class, I would like to bring them to the studio and discuss his paintings, how he started, his compositions and structural elements. I somehow think it would be more instructive to see the beginnings rather than finished work. Particularly, seeing the work of a famous painter solving the same problems that the students are confronting."

"I haven't let anybody in father's studio since he died."

"It would be a great treat for the students."

"I suppose it's time to stop keeping the windows closed. I'll say yes. Let me take you there now."

They crossed a large reception room adjoining Louisa's library, then a hall-way and a room beyond that. A small vestibule guarded the entry to Victor's studio. Louisa opened one of the carved double doors. She pulled back the canvas draperies obscuring the north studio window, another of Victor's large, composite windows, this with a gently arching top.

All the elements of the studio, ceiling, walls, floor, cabinets and canvas racks were painted a muted shade of white. The two white easels near the window each held a large, unfinished landscape. The canvas racks were full with more paintings, stacks in rows three high.

Louisa said, "I sold most of the finished pictures when father died. We had some expenses related to probate and the pictures were the only saleable asset. I'm sorry I don't still have them. They are worth a great deal more now than when he died. I am not interested in re-selling them, just having them back."

"I understand. A visit here would be the most valuable experience. Thank you for allowing it."

"Come by my office on the day of the class and I'll let you in."

Neil returned to his studio. He placed the canvas he had worked on in Galisteo on the easel and started to make additions and corrections. It was apparent that he and Victor started a painting in the same way, with red and raw sienna lines and solids. Neil had come upon this practice on his own in France, as it gave the finished work a sparkle when the small bits of red and sienna showed through.

# 14

# The Hand on His Knee

The next evening arrived without Neil's explanation to Sam. The day was over and the two were talking about the tribulations of their classes. Sam had a beer and Neil drank a glass of red wine. Sam said his students were lackluster and without promise and he did not see a single one capable of lighting a fire in a New York gallery.

Sam said, "Let's walk down to Canyon Road and get a bite."

"I can't. I'm having dinner with one of the students."

"Is that wise? What is her name?"

"It's not a her, it's a him".

"That is *really* not wise."

"He's an army veteran and we're the same age. He said he wants to be friends."

"I'll bet."

"He's from an old Santa Fe family, back here to help his father."

"None of this makes it better. I see trouble, Neil."

Just then Salazar knocked on their door. Neil let him in and introduced him to Sam, who muttered something unintelligible and went back to the bedroom with his beer.

Salazar said, "Wow. He's a bundle of charm."

"Sam's had a bad day."

"I'm not surprised if he treats everybody that way."

"Let's go, Salazar. I'm looking forward to the restaurant."

They drove to the Plaza in Salazar's small car. The ten-table café was on a side street leading off the Plaza. It was known for the reasonably priced diner fare. There were two other tables occupied, so they took the table at the far back.

Salazar said, "What do you want to drink?"

"I was drinking red wine with Sam. I'll just stick with that."

Salazar ordered and tested the wine. Then he asked Neil, "May I order for you?"

Neil said yes, but felt uncomfortable in this new, protected role, as if he were the student and Salazar the teacher. Salazar appeared to relish this reversal, pouring the wine to keep Neil's glass full.

Neil said, "You're a good host, but I just feel uneasy with such attention."

"It pleases me to make you happy."

"Let's just be friends and make each other happy."

"That sounds good to me."

"What are you going to do with a degree from the Monmouth School? Do you want to teach or just paint, be a working artist?"

"I don't know. I really have no definite plans for the future. Father pushes me to get married and have children; my sister has chosen her best friend for me. That's important in Catholic families. Then I can go on and do what I want."

"What is that?"

"What is what?"

"What you want."

Salazar took time to think about his answer. "The four years in Germany, away from Santa Fe, showed me that there were other things than being a dutiful son to a Catholic family. Things that I might like. I want to give the world a try. That's why I asked you to dinner."

"You want me to tell you about the world. I'm not sure I'm the one to ask." Neil was getting nervous about the direction of the conversation.

"You misunderstand. I'm sure that I know more about the world than you do. You may be a professor, but you have an innocence. A sweetness, underneath it all."

"How can that be?"

"Neil, I knew it when I first saw you. You're a good-looking, hot man, but I also saw a man not spoiled by experience. You're a sexual innocent. "

"I'm sort of the Anglo version of a Spanish virgin? The male version of your sister's friend?"

"You're making fun of me again. I'm serious."

"Me, too, I think."

"And, back to what I thought when I first saw you, I knew that you would eventually love me as much as I love you right now."

"That makes me really nervous," Neil said, not really surprised at Salazar's comment.

"Why? I can wait."

Neil felt trapped by his own emotions. Part of him wanted out of this conversation, but a stronger, older part of him wanted it to continue. Salazar had awakened something waiting, something inchoate that was now taking form. Neil thought with a smile that he had become nothing more than a male Sleeping Beauty.

Salazar said, "So, what do you think?"

"I think I need to go home and ponder bright with all my might."

"A virgin who's an overeducated smart ass."

"Sorry. When I get nervous, I try to be funny. I just naturally get out of difficult situations with what passes for humor."

"But I don't want you to get out of this situation."

"I know, Salazar."

They finished their dinner and walked around the Plaza, looking into the shop and gallery windows. Neil ran through what Salazar said and could not decide why he was so nervous about it. Despite the sameness of their ages, Neil felt much older. Salazar had, as he pointed out, more life experience in emotional matters. Neil's years of focusing on Sam had settled into a pattern of Neil being the one who constantly pursued. Sam offered the cheek, Neil kissed. To have that light focused back on himself was what made Neil uncomfortable, he was sure. The hand was on *his* knee, now.

Salazar said, "From the look of your face, you have troubled thoughts."

"I do."

"Do you want to share them?"

"No. But I will, when I've crunched through them and have an answer."

# 15

# To Please Someone Else

It was the day, now mid-November, of the class visit to Victor's studio. Neil had taken his six students on field trips to Galisteo and other sites, and an inside studio session would be perfect for this day that promised storms. Louisa unlocked the studio for the group, pulled back the canvas draperies, and left them alone in the large room.

The studio itself imparted a sense of importance to what Neil was about to say. Having a room this grand, this large investment of space wholly devoted to one purpose lent a sense of gravitas.

Neil said, "I looked at some of Victor Marriner's unfinished landscapes the other day. It occurred to me you could gain a lot in studying how he started to solve the problems we have talked about in Galisteo. Look here, for example."

Neil turned the easel around so that all six could see the Galisteo landscape that Victor had well under way. Like Neil's, it had a high horizon with the escarpment the major motif. These were well sketched in, Victor preferring to sketch details outside more completely than Neil. The outlines of the landscape features were in reds and in varying shades of green. He had started completing the forms in the middle of the canvas.

"What do you think made him stop at this point? A thunderstorm? Those cloud sketchings at the top of the canvas look threatening. Or was he just tired, ready to quit for the day? Something the next day prevented him from returning, so it stays this way."

Segunda said, "I would rather see more sky. Skies are so big and open here. Did he ever paint the skies as the main subject?"

Neil asked her, "I don't know. What do you think prompted him to cut out most of the sky?"

"He wanted to look at the ground?"

"I think so. Skies everywhere are almost the same, sometimes grander, sometimes more domestic, closer to the ground. But what he saw on the ground was unique to New Mexico, only to be seen in this Galisteo scene. If he had lessened that importance by including three-quarters sky with thunderheads and darkness, it would be quite a different painting."

Neil pulled a canvas at random from the shelves. It was a mountain scene of a cascading stream, rocks along the bank well-delineated with shadows and highlights, but the trees and grasses beside only sketched. Again Neil suggested that a summer rain had sent the painter scurrying away, running to the auto with the canvas held away from the drops.

"Look at the use of red in the sketching in. Some burnt umber here. Even a mostly green, summer mountain scene benefits from touches of red showing through."

The last he took out of the racks answered Segunda's question about skies. Here was a canvas with five-sixths of the composition a complicated design of a mackerel sky, small clouds scudding in lines across the sky. Victor had drawn in a horizon line in light purple, but nothing below.

"Since no storm threatened the painter here, he must have tired for the day, folded his easel and packed up. In his mind, he probably thought he could always insert something in the bottom of the picture to balance the movements of the sky."

Salazar said, "I like the canvases just the way they are."

"I do, too," Neil said. "There are some wonderful Cezanne paintings in a so-called unfinished state. But if the painting says everything the painter wanted to say, is it really unfinished? I am sure that if Victor were alive, he would finish these. Galleries pressure painters to give them completed works, as they sell easier. Only a name like Cezanne or Monet can support a market for uncompleted work."

Segunda said, "Should galleries be able to say when an artist is done? Is it always necessary to have paintings saleable, to make the galleries happy? Can't art just exist?"

"Certainly. Never paint to please someone else, gallery or buyer. On the other hand, it might be at cross-purposes with the function of art to make it pleasing to nobody else. If art is a language, there should be another person at the other end, to hear what it is you have to say."

The class continued discussing the canvases that Neil pulled from the racks. Some were very nearly done, only a corner of sky missing, others were little more than a sketch. Several hundred canvases lined the racks, and their mere presence gave Victor's studio an air of important intent.

As the class was drawing to an end, Louisa returned with an urgency about her. "Neil, I need to talk to you, please. Can you close up now?"

The class gathered their books and papers, moving quickly out, while Neil stayed behind.

Louisa said, "I just received a telegram from the embassy in Athens. Richard is dead." Her eyes filled with tears as she sat stiffly down in the easelside chair.

"What happened?"

"He drowned off Patmos a week ago, and they just found his body. The authorities there are waiting word for arrangements."

"Louisa, how terrible. I'm so very sorry." Her sorrow was right on the surface, a face holding back a flood of tears. Louisa was not a person Neil would think to hug for consolation, but he embraced her anyway. They stood together silently for a few moments, no words sufficient to express the sympathy.

He said finally, "Trafford Norwell told us how important Richard was to you. Do you want me to stay or is it right for you to be alone?"

"I thought I wanted to tell you first, I don't know why. Maybe I should be alone now."

Neil kissed her on the cheek and left her in her father's studio. Neil did not have a sister or a brother, but could he imagine how such a death would hurt? He did not know. It would surely cut more deeply than other deaths, to lose one you thought would always be there, a splinter in your generation gone.

# 16

# Potter's Field

At the end of the week, Lionel held a gathering of friends to commemorate Richard's death, opening the main room at Casa Marriner for the event. Richard's close friends from his Santa Fe youth had drifted away over the years, so the attendance was small. Despite never having actually met Richard, Neil, Sam and Carrie felt they should attend in respect for Louisa. Trafford Norwell and Harold were there, as well as Gloria Gallentine and a dozen townspeople.

Lionel attended the bar himself and Rita prepared a table of supper foods. After everyone who ought to be there appeared to have arrived, Lionel spoke a short memorial for Richard. Trafford read a poem, a long selection from Cavafy about solitary men on islands, looking westward to the mainland. Gloria's presentation rambled and went on so long that Lionel had to interrupt. Louisa did not speak. As the guests were departing, Lionel took Neil aside.

"Sad business, this. There are important and difficult ramifications that we must discuss. Can you come to my office?"

Neil waited there while the people cleared out and he could hear Lionel's low murmurings to Louisa. After several minutes he came in.

"Yesterday Louisa and I retrieved the will from the safe-deposit at the bank and we then walked across the Plaza to an appointment with the attorneys. Richard, of course, left everything to Louisa, including his half ownership in Casa Marriner."

"Why is that difficult?"

"The attorneys tell us that Louisa cannot avoid a high appraisal for the property at Casa Marriner this time. When Victor died years ago, Louisa and Richard were very lucky to slither like young minnows through the wide net of death taxes. Not so, this time, they claim."

Neil said, "So how much will they be?"

"The Camino del Monte Sol is no longer a quaint, dusty lane of artist cottages. Only fellow painters would live up here in Victor's time; goat pastures were good enough for painters, the locals said. Now the rich from the world over have sought out its rustic charm, elevating the worth of Casa Marriner considerably. The appraisal could be as high as three million. Dividing that in half for Richard's portion, the attorneys calculated that the tax on that could total half a million dollars, at the lowest"

"Can Louisa pay that?"

"Richard had no other assets, to speak of. The house on Patmos is worth very little, difficult to sell, and he had only a small portfolio. He lived on his book royalties. Louisa has some money laid aside, but not nearly enough for that iniquitous sum. She, of course, is devastated and fears she will have to sell Casa Marriner to pay for this inheritance."

"What a shame."

"She has nine months to sort things out, so this year at the Monmouth School is secure. I hate to think of the future beyond that. There is a further pressing matter I wanted to discuss with you, though."

"The lecture class. I know it's not going well because...."

Lionel frowned and interrupted. "That's not the matter I had in mind. Louisa must go to Patmos to arrange Richard's burial there. If she or some family member doesn't go, they must bury Richard in what amounts to a potter's field, ground unconsecrated by the Church. She is in no state for such negotiating, what with the estate problems. I would ask that you take care of this problem for her. I told her that you had experience traveling abroad and could arrange a proper, respectful internment in a foreign country better than anyone else I know. We will have papers drawn up giving you the needed authority. The school would, of course, pay all your expenses there and back."

"I would just leave my students and go?"

"Yes, the first semester is drawing to a close, anyway. I am sure Sam can double up and take your workshops for a couple of weeks. Carrie has already agreed to complete the lecture class. I must say, she has turned into a capable instructor. You'll be back by the time the second term starts in January."

"It sounds like it's already decided. How can I say no?"

"Splendid. I'll tell Louisa. You're a good son, Neil. I knew we could count on you."

"The dutiful child, once more."

Lionel heard the sarcastic tone. "The privilege of performing duty for ones you love is not to be taken lightly. Consider the alternatives. Consider yourself lucky."

Neil caught up with Sam and Carrie, who were waiting for him outside.

"I expect you know what's up. Lionel seems to have talked to you both."

Carrie said, "It's not a problem, Neil, taking over your lectures. I've learned to love talking about art and I can chatter on for hours. Sam's already figuring out how he can jigger the times around of his workshops for your morning field trips. It's all taken care of and Louisa won't have the funeral to worry about."

"I wish both of you were going, too. Even if it is not a happy trip, I'd be a lot easier if we were together."

"It will be winter in Greece. I've always heard that it's very rainy and nasty in the islands in winter. I guess you'll find out," Sam said.

"Lionel thinks I should go as soon as possible. He's having papers drawn up to give me power of attorney for Louisa, and when those are ready, I can go. Maybe day after tomorrow."

Sam said, "I wish I could go with you. If you're still there when Christmas break starts here, perhaps I can join you for a week or so."

"I would really like that, Sam."

"Carrie thinks I've not been paying enough attention to you, and Salazar is moving in to fill the void. Is that what's happening?"

"I don't know. Do I require that much maintenance?"

Carrie said, "We both think so. Since I told you about Sam's proposal of marriage, I think you've felt left out, somehow abandoned. Something in you feels that we will become a couple, a separate family and we'll completely disappear. That's definitely not the case."

"I don't feel abandoned. It seems the opposite, the busiest time of my life."

Sam said, "You should know that Carrie and I can't exist without you. Besides, how could a mere young stripling like Salazar fill my shoes? You told me in France that *I'm* the love of your life." Sam was learning Neil's knack of converting an important emotional turn into a humorous moment.

"You are, Sam." Neil had nothing more to say. His thoughts were as tangled as morning hair, so it was better to stay silent. He wondered, though, if it all was not the other way around, that Salazar's attention was a threat to them, making them feel ignored and abandoned. Whatever the nature of these risks, the threesome was in for a change.

# 17

# Purple Crocus

Neil's flight arrived in Athens just after noon. It was a still, chilly day with a brown cloud lurking over the city, the Parthenon almost obscured. He took a taxi from the airport to the downtown hotel that Lionel had recommended. It was a Neo-classic pile of carved stone on the main square and the rooms were a sad Nile green and noisy from the square's perpetual traffic.

Disoriented with the time change, he took a nap that afternoon, and awoke just as the sun was setting, deep orange through the haze. A travel agent's office was open on the square so he enquired about the ferries to Patmos. The winter schedule was twice weekly and he booked on the *Poseidon* leaving Piraeus at eight the next morning. It would be a six-hour trip to Patmos with stops along the way.

He walked into the Plaka and found a restaurant for dinner, maybe food would help his fuzzy mind. A few stalwart diners sat at the outside tables, but Neil chose a small table inside. The waiter brought him a glass of wine and waited for him to decipher the menu.

"Not many tourist at this time," he said.

"I'm going to Patmos tomorrow."

"Long trip. Cold on deck."

"This pollution, how long has it been around?"

"It comes and goes. It will go tomorrow."

After dinner, Neil went straight back to the hotel and spent a fitful night. He was packed and out early in the morning, a taxi to Piraeus. The waiter was right about the pollution, it had gone completely. Neil climbed up to the back deck of the ferry and watched the departure from harbor, the air so clear he could see all the way back to Athens.

It was cold on deck, but preferable to the smoky, crowded salon inside. Neil lay down on a bench out of the wind, covered himself with his coat and slept for four hours. He woke as the ferry was leaving a small island encrusted with a crown of white houses. He went in for a coffee and sandwich, and returned on deck to wait the arrival at Patmos.

The ferry docked in the small harbor of Skála, with clanks and halts as the ramp lowered; it was scheduled to return to Piraeus immediately. The sun was low in the sky, but the air was crisp, not cold as Neil walked along the stone quay to the center. Louisa had drawn a map to Richard's house, just on the other side of town. It was a "C" shaped harbor with the town in the middle, a large cathedral one street from the front.

He stopped in a small market and bought some oranges, bananas, wine and a loaf of bread. Richard's house was three blocks away and it was almost dark as Neil came to the entrance.

Louisa had described it perfectly: "You will see an ornate iron gate in the middle of a high iron fence, probably covered with vines by now. It is not one of those white-washed Cycladic cottages, but a cut stone, single-story Victorian town house with a garden, encircled by an impressive cast-iron fence with spear-like finials. Citrus, pomegranates and figs in the garden. Everything overgrown. Richard liked it that way."

The key she had given him worked on both the gate and front door. The stuffy aroma of the house was almost a second door, mildew and spices closing in strongly as he entered. The electric lights worked, so Neil turned on lamps and overhead lights, and opened the back door of the house for fresh air.

The house was amply furnished with heavy dark chairs and tables. Richard had clearly used the main room as his study since a long library table sat in the center with a green-glass shaded lamp, typewriter and stacks of books. There was a center hallway leading to a kitchen in the rear, two bedrooms and a single bathroom off to the left side.

What a strange house for the Greek islands, Neil thought. It would have been more at home in a Normandy village or the outskirts of Madrid. It was built before the turn of the century by a prosperous family, perhaps childless from the few bedrooms in the plan. He remembered Louisa using the word "Italianate." Perhaps it was built by bureaucrat from Naples who found the Aegean more agreeable than the crowded, dark streets of his home.

Neil turned on the lights in the kitchen. The water faucets in the sink ran rusty for a minute or so, then clear. He would drink the wine, instead. He poured himself a glass and walked out the kitchen door to the garden. It was too dark to identify the trees, but they crowded around the small terrace. He almost jumped when he turned around; a woman stood in the kitchen door.

"I'm sorry to startle you. I'm Alicia Carpenter, Richard's neighbor. You must be a relative."

"Hello, I'm Neil Bronson. Not a relative, but a friend of Richard's sister."

"I've been watching the house, knowing that someone would turn up."

"Louisa is very sad, as you must know."

"Such a bad business. Richard had become a good friend. My best friend, really. And I already miss him awfully."

"Tomorrow I'll look into providing Richard a proper burial. That's why I came."

"I can go along. My Greek isn't perfect, but I can make the locals understand me."

"That would help. I'm sorry, can I pour you a glass?"

"Yes, please."

Alicia was an English expatriate, she said, happy to be away from that horrid country of endless grey. She told Neil that she wrote and illustrated children's books with stories from a classical Greece long ago. She bought the house next door to Richard's ten years ago, moving from the more crowded Rhodes. Richard had become like a brother for her over the years.

"We swam together almost every day. The beach is half-a-kilometer that way, up a hill and down. I was always a stronger swimmer than Richard, but he could usually keep up. It was the start of every day for us, the walk to the beach and the morning swim. The winter months we stopped when the water temperature fell too low."

"How did he drown?"

"I don't really know. I was under the weather that day, and put him off. He said he would just take a short swim on his own, as it was getting cold.

That's the last I saw him alive. Three days later, they asked me to identify his body."

"Louisa says that authorities cannot allow him to be buried in church ground."

"We'll see about that tomorrow."

Alicia departed by the back garden, disappearing beyond a side gate. She told Neil that she would knock properly in the morning. The long days of travel had taken their toll and Neil felt a weariness descend like a curtain. He would unpack in the morning.

The bedroom was spare and monastic, with a narrow iron bed. Had Richard pulled up the sheets and spread on the morning of his last swim or had Alicia done that afterwards? Neil went immediately to sleep.

It was still dark when he woke. He found a coffeemaker in the kitchen and some ground coffee in the cupboard. He opened up the house to the fresh morning air, this time doors and windows, too. The windows opened with a squeaking complaint, so Neil knew that Richard was not an open-window type. Bookish, solitary and shuttered were the words that came to mind.

Neil looked around the house. Richard had a dozen or so of his father's paintings hanging around on the walls. Neil had not noticed them last night, but they gave a life to the rooms. Several of them were views of the Galisteo Basin where Neil had started his classes. Victor Marriner's paintings caught the bright, unusual colors of the place and made Neil feel suddenly homesick. A group of small forest scenes hung together in the hallway, the mountains above Santa Fe, but they could be conifer highlands anywhere in the world.

In about an hour, Alicia knocked at the side of the open kitchen door. Neil from the other room said to come in.

"I thought you might fancy a walk over to the water-front and a strong coffee by the sea before we face the Greek bureaucracy. Endless layers of angry clerks like some unpleasant, tart pastry. There's a reason the coffee here is as strong as it is."

"I would, indeed."

The cathedral doors were open as they passed, ranks of lighted candles shining from within. Alicia led him to a taverna facing the sun, outside tables set up against the wall's winter warmth. She ordered in Greek two coffees.

When they arrived, she said, "I anticipate we'll get a long run-around at the police offices. I've asked my Greek friends what to expect and they all say it will cost many fees and bribes to have his body sent back to America."

"Louisa thought that would be so."

"She understands the Greeks."

"Maybe the church officials can help."

"I doubt it. Richard was not a devout man and never, as I remember, even went into the cathedral for other than sightseeing."

"But maybe we should start there first."

They retraced their steps back to the cathedral, Neil depositing some drachmas and lighting a candle as they went in. Alicia led the way back to a door on the left and called something out in Greek in the vestibule.

A priest arrived through the far door and said something to her.

She said, first in Greek and then in English, "My friend here, Neil Bronson, has come especially to Patmos to bury his friend, Richard Marriner. You'll remember he drowned a month ago."

"Yes, yes. He was a foreigner, I thought. Had Richard taken confirmation in the Orthodox Church?"

"No, but he was a Christian and needs a proper burial, not in the potter's field."

"I can do nothing." His expression showed that nothing, in fact, would be done.

"Well, thank you, Father," Neil said. He gave the priest a stack of Greek currency and said, "Do you have any recommendations? Avenues that we can pursue?"

The priest motioned for them to sit down on the vestibule benches. He disappeared through the door and in a minute came back with a book in hand. He sat down a rifled though the pages, stopping at a place in the middle. He read for a while, and then said, "Did Marriner own a house on Patmos?"

Alicia said, "Yes, he was my neighbor."

"Do you know where the deed is?

"No, but I expect it is somewhere in his house. Why?"

"These are the laws of the Greek Republic. Any man who owns his own land can be buried on it. It doesn't happen often, because most want to be in consecrated ground. The early republicans were often atheists and demanded this provision. The church has no official reponse to this."

Alicia said, "Thank you, father. Would you write down the name and number of that law?"

He did and Neil added to the previous drachma notes. Armed with that, they went to the constabulary on the other side of the harbor. Alicia, in prime Englishwoman-abroad form, demanded and got immediate approval for the release of Richard's casket that afternoon, to be buried in his own garden. Neil saw why the British Empire made such inroads all over the world.

Outside, Neil said, "I am sure Louisa would agree. She had hoped Richard could be buried in blessed ground, but possibly we can get the father to say a prayer."

"We must locate that deed before they will actually release the body, however."

"I will tend to that."

Alicia said, "I notice you have a delicate understanding of the Greek love of a little money to grease the wheels. The mayor's office would screech to a stop without it."

"They are not so different from the French. In Gordes they call it 'the gift with heart.'"

Back at the house it was a short hunt for the necessary paper. Richard's filing cabinet had a folder devoted solely to "Deed." Neil, without Alicia, took it to the constabulary. A clerk, whom Neil paid with more drachmas, took twenty minutes to copy the information into a large book. He prepared another paper, stamped it with several stamps, and permission was granted. He stopped at the cathedral on the way back, and the priest would say a simple, non-denominational prayer. Drachmas again.

Neil realized he could not have organized this solution without Alicia. She knew several Greek men who retrieved Richard with a small truck, the casket hanging out over the end, covered with ropes. Wooden crates of cabbages, bottled water and vegetables temporarily adorned the top of the casket.

Alicia said to Neil, "I think the back garden is the proper place. Next to that large fig in the back corner. Richard loved those figs and would, I know, spend eternity happily in their company."

It was a bright, sunny afternoon for their unpretentious ceremony. The two men lowered the coffin with ropes into the grave they had dug. The priest recited the short prayer he found suitable for foreign infidels and bid them good afternoon. Alicia and Neil gently dropped the last roses from the garden onto the casket and she read a poem in Greek. When the grave was refilled and tamped, the men left. More drachma.

Alicia said, "I can still buy crocus at a shop in town and plant them here. The purple crocus, I think, as Richard and I always looked forward to their bloom over in the churchyard."

"I will let Louisa know how you've managed this so well. She will, I know, be pleased that her brother is safely in the ground."

"So am I."

The next day, autumn storms returned with winds and cold rain; the impatient gods of winter could wait no longer. The ferry to and from Athens was cancelled, as well as the one scheduled for the beginning of next week. Sam's prediction about Greek island weather proved to be accurate. Neil booked a ticket for a Piraeus ferry leaving in nine days.

He spent the time reading from Richard's library, history books and biographies of Greek scholars. When the sea squalls broke for brief intervals, he took his sketchbook out and drew the buildings, trees and streets of Skála. A shop in town stocked a whole shelf of Italian sketchbooks, parchment-thick papers bound in fine brown leather. He came back to buy a new one several times, as the former purchase filled with his India ink drawings.

Evenings were spent with Alicia, either at her house for a simple meal or at a favorite taverna on the quay. At first impatient to be off the island, Neil fell into the slow pace of a Patmos winter. He began to sleep well and felt rested.

One evening, Alicia said, "You must come back to Patmos in the spring or fall. You will love it as much as Richard did. Winter is not a fair sample."

"I've grown to like the island off-season. I will return in the summer, however, and I would like to bring my friends, Carrie and Sam."

"I have two spare rooms. All of you can stay with me."

"Louisa will sell the house, I presume. She needs the money to pay the death taxes, so be on the lookout for a buyer."

"I'll hate that, having new people in Richard's house."

"It can't be helped. Thank you for the invitation to stay with you. I feel that I've made a good friend in you, Alicia, and I am sure I will take you up on that."

Finally, the day of departure came. It was overcast, but not so stormy that ferry cancellations were imposed. Alicia accompanied Neil down to the water end of the dock to await the ferry. She had told him everyone returning to Athens waited there, as the ferry did not tarry very long after out-coming passengers were disembarked.

"I'll miss you, Neil. In a way, your stay has bridged that awful loneliness in those weeks right after Richard's death. Your being here has made it all easier."

"I will let you know about when we can return."

The ferry's horn sounded as it rounded the promontory, rushing to shore. The ramp came down and one truck and several people descended.

Neil hugged Alicia and turned to go up the ramp.

He suddenly recognized the last passenger, with a large backpack, coming down the ramp. It was Sam.

# 18

# The Narrow Grassy Trail

Neil dropped his pack and hugged Sam with a hard delight. It was a moment of confusion as he told the ferry captain he would not be using his ticket today.

"Sam, I can't believe you're here. I am delighted."

"I couldn't have you face everything here alone."

"I haven't actually been alone. Alicia, here, made it all possible."

Alicia put out her hand and Neil said, "This is my Sam, about whom I talked so much."

They shook hands and the three walked back down along the quay to Skala. Neil excitedly told Sam a short version of Richard's retrieval and burial as they walked. Alicia sensed a new dynamic in Neil, one that did not include her or Patmos, and she excused herself, saying that she needed to go by the market. She would come by Richard's house tomorrow.

After Neil opened up the house and found a glass of wine for each of them, he said. "Curious house, isn't it?"

Sam said, "It reminds me of those on the outskirts of Gordes. I wouldn't have picked it for Greece."

"How is Carrie?"

"All right. She wanted to come, too, but her father said she was needed in the bosom of her family in New York for Christmas."

"Why doesn't that surprise me? How are you?"

"I'm a little blinky with the travel. Greece is a lot farther than France. And a bumpy ferry trip out to the island just adds another day to it."

"Beautiful, though, don't you think?"

"If you like forgotten islands in the middle of cold water. You can't get enough of the waterside, can you?"

"Since the next ferry is two days after Christmas, we'll spend the holiday here."

"I didn't want you to be alone, so that's why I came."

Neil put sheets and a blanket on the bed in the second bedroom, while Sam unpacked. There was no closet, but an oak wardrobe held everything from Sam's pack with room to spare. They sat down at the kitchen table.

"So tell me how things are in Santa Fe."

"Carrie's fine, as I said. Louisa has settled down after the news about Richard and the estate problems. She doesn't have a solution, but at least she's not freaked out by it anymore. I think Lionel has worked to calm her."

"How did the field trips go?"

"Interesting, to say the least. Trafford gave me some other locations for the trips. We spent a week up in the Sangre de Cristos, before the worst of the snows arrived. We spent another week in Diablo Canyon west of the town. That turned out well."

"Which of the students did the best, do you think?"

"Ollie Bainbridge and I connected. He's turning into a good, traditional painter. And Segunda. She's a strange young thing, but I like her work. Strong and different.."

"I liked what I saw of her painting."

"Did you know her mother is a very successful painter in New York? A second rank abstract impressionist. She came to visit Santa Fe and went out with us one day. Sat in a folding chair, dressed all in black and watched from under a black umbrella. Like a big raven. I liked her, but it is clear that Segunda is terrified of her."

"What about Salazar?"

Sam scratched his head and said, "He and I have a problem. We clashed about everything, where we would go, when to leave, where to set up the easels, you name it."

"I can understand."

"He wants you, not me, to teach him. He was always asking me what I thought Mister Bronson would think? When were you going to get back? There's more than student-teacher there, Neil."

"I know. Perhaps I'm to blame for that."

"You are, I can assure you."

Neil was not ready to tell Sam what he thought about Salazar. He was not really ready to tell himself, so he said, "What about your own work in the studio?"

"Going well. I have six finished, working on two more. Segunda's mother came by to see them, but she didn't make any comments, just spent a long time looking as I unfurled one after the other. She said that when I was done with them she would tell me where to send them."

"That could an important introduction."

"We'll see. Gallery connections have a way of disappearing when you need them. By the way, our exhibit with Hetty's gallery in London was a mixed success. We each sold three paintings. Carrie talked to her on the day after the opening, so maybe a few more have sold by now. No reviews as yet."

"So our futures don't lie in landscape painting? I think we knew that anyway."

"I've decided that I really like to work in a studio, no flies to swat, no wind to knock the easel over."

"I'm proud of you, Sam. You've done with Santa Fe exactly what we discussed last summer, used it as a stepping stone to New York. Your decision was right."

"I do have something else to tell you. Carrie accepted my proposal and we will be married this summer in New York. She's going to look for a loft, a place for me to paint and us to live."

"That's great, Sam. Carrie is a lucky woman," Neil's eyes telling Sam of the mixed feelings behind them.

After that they called it a night and went to bed. Neil could hear that Sam's heavy breathing coming from the other bedroom. Not so for Neil.

The next day was Christmas Eve and Alicia had invited them to an expatriate's dinner at her house, including some other island exiles. It was not the Greek Orthodox Christmas, but it was nice to be an island on an island.

The fair weather continued with no sign of rain or winds, only a crisp, winter air. Neil gave Sam a long walking tour of Skala, looking into the cathedral and the honeycomb of narrow streets back from the harbor. All the shops and tavernas were closed and shuttered, businessmen celebrating both holidays with a locked door.

That night, Alicia said to Sam, "I have a favor to ask of you. I want you to convince Neil to come back here this summer, when the Aegean is warm and clear and the days cloudless, one after the other. He will savor it fully, and I expect you will, too. I want to get Patmos into your blood."

"He will love it, Alicia. More than me. He's a Mediterranean nut and told me he knows he will end up living somewhere along its shores. I think his grandmother told him that early on and he hasn't forgotten."

"Good. I need all the help I can get. But you and your new wife must come here too.'

"I'm really a city dweller."

"I was, too, before Greece. Now I'm a devoted hermit. And in the burning summers here, the waters beckon their cool welcome. It's the autumns that I like the most, when the sea turns imperceptibly cooler each day, a luscious withdrawal. Patmos is the ideal place for a writer or an artist."

"Neil said you helped him a lot."

"I was glad to. He's an extraordinary young man. But you already know that."

"I love Neil, totally and completely. I can't tell him that in person, because it will make his head big."

"You should. It would mean a great deal to him. From the vantage point of great age, I know it is better to say things than not to say things. Without exception."

"I'll consider that."

Alicia had said her piece, so she moved on to other subjects. "Tomorrow, you and Neil must hike over to the beach. There is a narrow, grassy trail from there up to Hora and the monastery. You can see everything on the island from there."

"We will. We have a few days to fill before the ferry back."

The next morning, Christmas Day, remained clear and bright. After coffee in the morning, they walked over to the beach, ten minutes away. It was a small cove with sand of a light raw sienna, shading to a deeper hue in the transparent, cold waters.

Neil said, "This is where Richard drowned. Right out there."

"Lonely place."

"It seems beautiful to me."

"I know. You're strange that way."

The found the path to Hora. It followed the shore for a while, then climbed slowly up along a rocky slope. Although there were trees elsewhere on the island, this section had only grasses and shrubbery undergrowth, now bright green from the rains. The monastery of St. John sat in the middle of the village, with small streets of white houses clinging like barnacles to the outside walls.

Every place of business in the village was closed. They passed by the main ramp up to the monastery doors and walked over to a small promontory with a lookout over the island.

"I think you can see Turkey over there, just beyond that other island. The beginning of Asia." He pointed off to the east. The neighboring islands dappled the sun-white sea with a clear blue line low on the horizon.

"I see why you like it, Neil."

"I'm sure I'll be back here."

"I think so, too."

In two days they boarded the ferry back to Piraeus with Alicia waving from shore as they departed. The boat left Skala in the late afternoon and deposited them on the mainland around midnight. The taxi to the hotel on the square took another hour.

Neil and Sam stayed in Athens for two days in the continued cloudless weather of midwinter. Winds from the north blew away the orange-brown cloud and they walked the central streets of the city. Neil knew that Sam was being especially soliticitous, often strolling with his arm over Neil's shoulders.

They stopped to look at the view from the Acropolis. Sam said, "I want you to come with us to New York. Carrie is looking for a loft large enough for the three of us, a studio for you and one for me. Your delight in Santa Fe won't last."

"I know you're right. But you and Carrie will need a place of your own."

"We both want to make room for you, to make you a home with us. I've told you plenty of times, you are part of me."

Even if he did not believe it anymore, it was what Neil wanted to hear. "Thanks, Sam. I feel the same."

"You know that Carrie would rather marry you than me. It doesn't bother me that she will always love you more."

"It can't be, though."

Sam said, "I feel strange about that, as though I had inherited a fortune that actually belongs to you."

Their flight home went through London, with a connection in Chicago and back to Albuquerque at midnight. Neil was awake in the taxi as it crested the last hill to the valley that held Santa Fe, a cluster of lights against the mountains, this remote outpost that had claimed part of him. He wondered if Sam was right and he would tire of this small town with glittering lights in long rows.

# 19

# The Dollar Will Fall

It was matriculation day for the spring term and students clustered around the tables in Lionel's large salon. Snow was on the ground outside and the crowd arrived with much stamping and scraping in the entrance hall. Neil's lecture class was cancelled by Lionel, who took pity on both the teacher and his students, he said. Instead, Neil would have three separate classes of *plein air* workshops, word having passed that they were not the bore that first term students expected them to be.

The curriculum at Lionel's school was totally voluntary; students could take any course they wanted, so long as they did not avoid his seminar on Aesthetic Considerations. Salazar wanted to sign up for two of the *plein air* workshops, but Neil tried to veer him into other courses.

"Why don't you try Trafford Norwell's portrait class? It meets at the same time."

Salazar said, "I would rather go out with you."

Neil took the double meaning, but said, "And why not Gloria Gallentine's class in the modern canvas? She could give you something in the way of contemporary design and scale. Or Eisenhart's course in the large painting? It's the most popular class in the school."

"Not this year."

"What about more of Sam's studio techniques? He knows a lot about paints and how to use them."

"I'm only interested in landscape painting and you."

"Fair enough. I'll sign you up for both."

Both Segunda and Ollie committed to another term, which pleased Neil enormously. If he could influence only three students in one year, to really give them an insight to what he thought about the subject, it would not be all in vain. Neil looked forward to the start of classes in two days.

Back at the Roman Studio that afternoon, he started on some of his own work at the big easel. He had an idea about large paintings of the Galisteo River; looser, more abstract panels of the bright earth colors. He brought out some of his small paintings and sketches and used them to start a studio version. It would be more considered, less in the rush of emotion that work outdoors encouraged.

As the work on the canvas grew, he became more absorbed in the project and painted all afternoon. It was dark outside when he finally stopped. The painting had taken shape and now he could see a way to the end. He wrote down a list of what to do with the painting when he returned to it:

*1. Mitigate the reds in the escarpment*
*2. Work on horizon...much lighter, more violet*
*3. Foreground reworked, more shadow and light.*
*4. Pinons need a line of dark and light.*
*5. Darken, lighten everywhere*
*6. Leave drips and splatters*

Sam returned to the studio after an afternoon with Carrie downtown. He said, "We're walking down to Canyon Road for dinner. Want to join us?"

"Yes. I'll be ready in a minute."

"You've got some good painting done. I should leave you alone more often."

"I like it, too. Maybe the beginning of a series."

They walked the few blocks down to the restaurants on Canyon Road and picked the one that looked empty. They ordered and Carrie said, "I've got good news for both of you."

Neil said, "Is it about New York?"

"Yes, but first about London. Hetty called today, and she has almost sold out your exhibit and opened bank accounts in London for each of you. I told her to do that. I hope you don't mind. You can spend the money over there or you can transfer it here. My father thinks it would be wise to keep it in British pounds for now, as the dollar will fall."

"I don't mind, at all."

"Of course, she now wants more South of France paintings, wants you to spend your summer there. I told her I was not sure about that."

"A nice change from a year ago. What's the news about New York?"

"Father has found a loft and it's large enough for a separate apartment for you, Neil."

"Everything is falling into place, it seems."

"You don't sound happy about it."

"I am happy. It's what we've wanted."

Sam and Carrie could hear the doubt in Neil's voice. Thinking better of pursuing an interrogation, Sam changed their conversation to students and the school. They did not return to the topic of New York again that evening.

The next day Neil's field trip set up on Lamy Hill overlooking the expanse of the Galisteo Basin, a tapestry of snow, pinons and earth colors. The students stamped their feet and clapped their hands against the cold. They were clearly excited about facing a motif in disagreeable weather, chill winds from the west requiring that they weight down the easels with rocks. Neil had regaled them on the bus with stories about Monet strapping down his easel in the coastal winds of Normandy and Victor Higgins crawling with a canvas into the trunk of his car to avoid the snowfall.

By the time Neil got around to Ollie's easel, he had already sketched in a complex view of the whole valley, with river, crestons and long drifts of native vegetations. Neil was impressed with the growth of his expertise since last year.

"You've come a long way, Ollie. I like it."

"Thanks, Mister Bronson. I've been using your high horizon and it works."

"You're making it work."

Segunda's painting looked the opposite direction at a closely cropped juniper and snow compostion. Her canvas was more concerned with the colors in the violet-blue shadows than the juniper itself, and no sense of distance and horizon. It was totally an exercise in foreground detail, more of her introspective take on the landscape.

"Even your mother might like that. It's more abstract and non-objective."

"Don't tell her, please. I want to surprise her with it."

Salazar made the most progress since Neil had last seen his work. He divided the valley view into triangles and angles as seen through the facets of a cut gem stone. Neil thought of John Marin. Salazar's version was not forced, but a natural attempt to organize the landscape into acceptable parts.

"I'm impressed. Did you spend time in the downtown museum over the holidays?"

"Yes. You recognize the Marin? I want to make it my own, though. Not copy what he saw."

"You'll need to rise to another level, then, because it looks very like Marin as it is. It is okay to copy when you're a student. When you master his approach, you can go on, find your own way of painting things. It's important to find that."

Salazar watched Neil was he was talking, not really listening. "Can we have dinner again, soon.? And what about our painting out here together this week end?"

"Yes, to both. It will be my turn for dinner. On Saturday?"

"Great. I'll come by your studio at seven and pick you up."

"I'll like that, being picked up."

# 20

# Two Percent

When Neil returned to his studio, he found an envelope with his name under the cast-iron door knocker. It was from Louisa Marriner, a letter asking him to come by her office anytime in the afternoon. After a quick lunch of sandwich and milk at the studio, he walked over to the main building.

Louisa was in her library. She got up when Neil came in and directed him to a pair of chairs across from her desk.

She said, "I'll say again how much I appreciate your going to Patmos."

"It was a sad journey, Louisa, but I believe even Richard would have approved of the way it worked out."

"I think it was the perfect solution. He would not have liked being in a churchyard forever and ever. I think about poor Alicia. She and Richard supported each other and, I am sure, loved each other. She will miss him, even more than me."

"I didn't have a time to describe my respect for your father's paintings in Richard's house. How completely expressive of New Mexico they are. They made me quite homesick."

"You must notice the great similarity with what you are doing now and Father's work of thirty years ago. Just yesterday I saw the paintings at Carrie's house. At first, I thought that Carrie had found and purchased some lost pictures of Father's. They were yours, of course."

"That's quite a compliment, as Victor's work is so outstanding."

"Father avoided the Academy approach to painting and came up with his own, distinctive style. You have done the same; two men arriving at nearly the same place by different roads."

"I've started in another direction, just today. Bigger paintings, more abstracted but still with the landscape as the center."

She said, "The technique that you have mastered is virtually the same that served Father for most of his life. It's that style I want to talk to you about. As you know, he left several hundred unfinished paintings."

"I showed many of them to the students, and we all felt that they had great power and direction, even unfinished."

"Regrettably, unfinished paintings have very little market value. When I have consulted several galleries downtown, I said that among the many paintings Father left me, there were some unfinished. I thought it unwise to give the exact ratio. Each gallery owner said the same. An unfinished canvas is a hard sell for anything other than the very top echelon of painters, such as those wonderful Cezannes and Lautrecs. I am not deluded in the matter. Father was a fine, regional painter, but not a member of that top, international rank."

"Why does it matter? They will end up in a museum collection as they are."

"Penrose Gallery has offered to stage an auction of a group of paintings to help me pay for the estate taxes on Casa Marriner. A successful auction could pay for a large percentage of them."

"You must ask Alicia to send you those in Richard's house. They were among his best."

"I've thought of that, but they, with the few in the studio that are complete, don't add up to enough to make an auction worth it. I need about twenty more of comparable value. That's where you come in, Neil."

"What do you mean?"

"I have spent several mornings going over the paintings in the studio. There are forty or so which are virtually done, only lacking a sky or some small corner. I asked Penrose, in general terms, about these and he said they would still be viewed as unfinished."

"Louisa, are you suggesting that I work on these paintings?"

"Yes. Please don't say no right off the bat."

"Wouldn't that be illegal?"

"You would not be signing his name, only doing what most would consider to be restoration work."

"But what about the technology of uncovering fakes?"

"I don't think that is a problem. Father himself purchased all the paints, brushes and solvents that are now in his studio, so everything would be authentic and of the period. Even the canvases on which they are painted are all at least thirty years old. I would not ask you to finish the sketchy ones, only the canvases that are ninety-eight percent there already."

"So it's only a two-percent fraud? I'll have to say no."

"Please wait and think."

"Give me a few days, Louisa. However, I think you'd better be prepared for a no."

She said, "It would make the difference in whether we lose the school and Casa Marriner, or not."

"You shouldn't put that heavy load on me, alone."

"I have no choice, Neil. The forty paintings could bring twenty thousand or more each. It would get us out from underwater."

Neil gave her a forced smile and left. What a predicament, he thought. If he did not agree, the school would be lost and he would be the villain. If he did agree, what degree of a felon would he be? Is a two-percent trickster any better than a ninety-eight percent one?"

# 21

# An Undivided Half

Louisa had not returned a call from Gilbert Overton, a local real estate investor and developer of office rentals throughout the Southwest. An unsavory reputation preceded him, so Louisa put off the return call. It seemed a strong possibility that Neil would not go along with her scheme, but after thinking about it, she dialed the number.

"I would like to talk to Gilbert Overton. It's Louisa Marriner."

"I'll put you right through."

There was a wait of half-a-minute, then, "Hello, Miss Marriner. I'm glad you returned my call."

"Yes."

"As you might have determined, my call is about your property called Casa Marriner."

"Yes."

"My attorney, Pernell Snopes, tells me that the clock is ticking on inheritance taxes. I thought I might be able to help you out."

"I didn't know that death taxes were public knowledge."

"They aren't. Mister Snopes got word through his most confidential sources. I would be prepared to make you an offer for an undivided half interest in Casa Marriner. Would you prefer I wrote you or can we talk?"

Who were these confidential sources? Surely nobody at the school had spread the word around. "We can talk."

"Very good. I will, naturally, follow this up with a formal offer, but I will pay you a half a million dollars cash for a simple undivided half interest in the property."

"I'm not sure I know what undivided means."

"It means that we would each own fifty percent of the whole property and not you one specific half and me the other half."

"It seems like a very low offer from the appraisal price I am working with."

"That appraisal would be the retail price. I never pay a retail price for real estate investments, and I would call my proposal a good Samaritan price. What I offer would more than pay your taxes and get you out of the jam."

"I don't know that I am actually in a jam, as you describe it."

"I have it on best authority that you are. Banks are very loathe to make loans now unless you have a similar amount on deposit. The good name of the borrower, even as good as yours, amounts to little. The bankers are the villains, not me."

Louisa sighed and realized where Overton got his information. The banker she confided in last week, who had, with much understanding, turned her down and did not honor the confidentiality of her request. "I will let you know, Mister Overton. I can't make the decision over the telephone."

"I understand. Thank you, Miss Marriner."

So the carrion birds were circling. If Overton knew, then others did as well. Louisa realized she would have a hard time getting a good price for Casa Marriner when potential buyers knew her plight. Even though she hoped that she would not be compelled to accept Overton's offer, it meant that Casa Marriner might be saved.

She walked across to Lionel's office. He was not there. She walked over to his house and knocked. After a very long wait, Lionel came to the door.

"Come in, dear. I was napping between seminars."

"Do you have a moment to talk?"

"Are there developments?"

"I've received an offer from Gilbert Overton. He wants to buy a half interest in Casa Marriner. An *undivided* half interest."

"That sounds dangerous. Overton has a reputation for making life very unhappy for his partners. He is known for buying an undivided half interest from an owner under stress. Then, when problems appear of any sort, he refuses to agree to whatever the others want. He, alone, can stop anything, like a building permit or any change, howsoever small. Eventually, he buys the other partner out, who gives in for what they call 'a song,' just to stop the annoyance. Overton is very successful."

"I know you disapprove, but I asked Neil to work on the unfinished canvases. He said he would think about it. At least, that's another potential way out. If Neil agrees, that is."

"Not an honorable way, I'm afraid. I would rather lose the school than have Neil take on a dishonest project. It appears all our solutions have a dubious quality about them."

"Very disagreeable, both."

"I advise you to do nothing now. A third way will appear, I am sure."

"As that reptile, Overton, says, with a great deal of joy in his voice, the clock is ticking."

"I will bring it up at the faculty dinner, tonight. Perhaps we have missed something that is obvious and one of our people has the solution."

# 22

# Without Options

Lionel prepared for the faculty evening, polishing the cocktail glasses with a dry towel and arranging the bottles. His left hand had developed an annoying tremble which made the process more difficult. What a time for infirmity to raise its head. Rita had already set the table and tended to a standing roast in the kitchen. As the aroma of cooking filled the house, the host in him came to the forefront and the tremble settled down. Knowing it was Louisa who would knock first, he went to the door.

"Welcome, my dear. You must ignore all my advice today on the subject of taxes and do what you think best. I have no right to tell you what you must or mustn't do. I don't know why I am such a meddler."

"I value your advice. Don't stop giving it, please."

"I have a notion that something will come to light tonight."

"Like what?"

"Some solution, some elegant answer to your plight. Something we haven't thought of before, just lying in wait for its own discovery."

"We'll see, Lionel. Meanwhile, a vodka, please."

The others started to arrive, first Eisenhart and Bella, then Gloria Gallentine.

Gallentine said, "Lionel, I smell a roast, you devil. Squandering school money on the appetites of insiders again."

He replied, "I was almost sure that no one would fully appreciate Rita's inestimable fried fish again or her prized enchiladas. So a roast it is. With Yorkshire Pudding, no less."

"With such a menu, I can't wait for the after dinner talk."

"Wait-And-See Pudding, as they say."

Trafford Norwell and the three young instructors arrived together in a group. The room soon filled with talk and the sound of cocktails clinking in their glasses. Louisa sought out Neil and asked if they could talk confidentially away from the others.

She said, "I was so wrong this afternoon to pressure you."

"I understand your worry."

"Please pay no attention to what I said. Lionel told me that it was unethical and impossible for me to ask you such a thing."

"Thank you, Louisa. I will ignore it."

In a few moments, Eisenhart sidled up to the two of them and put his arm around Neil's shoulders. Neil flinched at bit, knowing that a familiar gesture from Eisenhart quite often meant exactly the opposite.

"What are you two plotting? You both look guilty."

"Guilty of having a good time," Neil said.

Eisenhart raised his eyebrows and said, "What a glib answer. Why do I doubt that? Anyway, I wanted to tell Louisa that the cat is out of the bag on your estate problems. I talked to Gilbert Overton just an hour ago and he told me about his offer."

Louisa said, "You and Overton are friends?"

"Let's say we have common interests."

"I will probably turn him down. Your information is incomplete."

"Why don't you fill Neil here in on the contents of the offer."

She looked at Neil, "Overton offered to pay me enough to settle the taxes if I give up half ownership in Casa Marriner. An undivided half."

"Is that something you would do?"

"Perhaps it's not necessary. I have other options."

Eisenhart said, "Overton claims that you are without options. He thinks his success is only a matter of time. He is a steamroller when he wants something."

She said, "I do hope that is not so."

Lionel soon announced dinner and they all sat down in their assigned places. Louisa was on Lionel's right, as usual, and she thought about what Eisenhart had said. She must talk quietly with Lionel after the dinner. Things could be getting out of hand.

The conversation did not include mention of Overton, but matters of instruction and art instead. After Lionel's State of the School speech, he said, "Now, I propose we openly discuss what is on everybody's mind, the matter of how to pay for the inheritance taxes that cloud the future here. Would anyone like to propose something on that subject. We are, after all, the ones most concerned with happenings here."

The guests looked around at their neighbors, awaiting the first to speak out. It was Eisenhart who did, standing up and taking a position behind his chair.

"I, for one, believe that Gilbert Overton's offer, which we actually all know about, should be accepted. It quickly stops this time of uncertainty and questioning, and is, on the whole, a fair offer. He has have kindly asked me to be his *eminence gris,* as it were, so I could see that business continued as usual."

Lionel felt a pang of alarm. "Please expand on your proposed role in this, Randolph."

"Gilbert Overton would create a new position for me here, which I suggested could be Chancellor. It would be over and above the existing hierarchy. It seems only right it should be somebody already here, someone who knows the foibles and dark corners of the school."

Louisa could take no more. She stood up and said, "Lest this go any further, you must know that I have *not* agreed to Gilbert Overton's offer. We only today talked. I can't think what profits the telephone company has made this afternoon alone; their lines must have been burning."

Gloria said, "Louisa, dear, it's the only answer. You will accept in time. The Overtons, and particularly Apricot Overton, are big collectors of my work and they are darling. I recommend acceptance."

"We'll see. I think Lionel was hoping for *other* solutions than the Overtons when he asked for comment. Does anybody have one?"

Silence, interrupted after a minute by Lionel.

He said, "I am deeply shocked how disloyal, verging on traitorous, some of our people are. All this talk behind the arras is most upsetting. I will personally assist Louisa in finding other ways to satisfy this obligation. Dinner is over."

As the guests picked up their coats and said goodnight with forced smiles to Lionel and Louisa, Neil waited until they had gone. Lionel went into the kitchen to confer with Rita.

"Louisa, I've changed my mind. The unfinished paintings might be the better solution."

"No, if you don't feel right about it."

"I feel a lot righter than I did before this dinner."

"We'll talk about it tomorrow."

"I think that you might sleep better knowing that I will definitely go ahead with your project.

Louisa gestured to Neil to sit down on the bench by the front door. She said, "Thank you, my dear. You have once again made my life easier. Why did you decide that?"

"As I heard Eisenhart and Gloria describe the Overton crowd, it made me shudder to think what people like that can do to the fragile balance at Lionel's school. My ability as a painter is my power to resolve this. I cannot refuse."

"It must be totally secret. Only Lionel and I know about it. Your friends and the students must be completely it the dark, you understand?"

"I do."

# 23

# The Martinez Daughter

Easter was a well-celebrated feast day in Santa Fe, both the early and noon masses filling the cathedral to capacity. The local families marked the rest of the day with banquets, friends as well as family invited. Salazar invited Neil and Segunda Plaith to his family's dinner at the Ortega family house on a northside hill. Salazar's father, Procopio Ortega, built the house in the years right after World War II, a sprawling Territorial design.

Salazar had already collected Segunda when he came by Neil's studio. She waited in the car while he went to knock. Sam answered the door.

"Mister Bonifacio. Happy Easter."

"Hello, Salazar. Neil will be right here. It could take him a minute or so. Do you want to invite Segunda in?"

"No." He waved to Segunda that it would be a few minutes.

"Good, because I have something to talk to you about. It's about Neil, of course."

"Yes. I've become very fond of Neil, as you know."

Sam said slowly, for effect, "I love Neil like a brother. As I see the two of you spending more time together, I wonder if you love him that way, too?"

"I do, Mr. Bonifacio. We are a lot alike, you and me."

"I must warn you to be careful with his love. He is very fragile, in my mind, and I would hate to see him hurt. Am I clear?"

Salazar could not resist a smile at the protectiveness implied in Sam's statement. It could be that Sam's love was as different from that of a brother as his was. "Very clear."

Neil appeared out of the bedroom and said, "*Listo*, Salazar? I could hear Sam from the other room and I'm lucky to have such an earnest guardian."

"*Si.* Goodbye, Mr. Bonifacio," Salazar said, still with his smile.

Sam watched at the door as they left.

It was a short trip to the Ortega house, now brimming with family and family friends. Salazar introduced the two guests to his father, who stood near the door to the entry hall.

"Father, this is Segunda Plaith, my favorite other student and Mister Bronson, my most favorite teacher. I am taking two of his landscape classes."

"Welcome, both of you. Mister Bronson, Salazar cannot stop talking about your course and how much he likes it. And you, of course."

"Salazar and Segunda are both excellent students. I am lucky to have them."

"Please introduce your friends to everybody, Salazar." Procopio watched Neil closely as he walked into the main sitting room.

Neil looked around the room and took in the full assortment of the Ortegas, most black-haired and dark-eyed, unlike Salazar's red-headed looks. The Ortega family face came from Old Spain, the face that Velasquez painted again and again. Neil thought that the Prado had come alive and here for Easter dinner. An elegant, older woman came forward and welcomed them.

Dinner was served at a very long table in a separate dining room. Procopio made a point of seating Neil nearby, so he could talk about Salazar.

"Mister Bronson, my older brother was an artist. I have some of his work, which I treasure, in my office. Placido was killed in Verdun in World War One."

"I'm so sorry. Salazar will continue his tradition, then."

"I'm hoping so. I was too young to serve, but we planted apple trees in his memory afterwards."

"Here at the house?"

"No, at Casa Marriner. It was called Casa Ortega, then."

"So Casa Marriner was your family home? Salazar never told me that. It's a lovely place and I do know where the apple trees are. There was a large crop last fall."

"Salazar cannot remember it as home the way I do. He was born after we sold it and only knows about it from family stories."

"Did you sell it to Victor Marriner?"

"He bought it from us in the Depression. We had to sell. He paid our full price in cash and that was the single act that saved the family from ruin. I have always respected Mister Marriner. We had the resources to get through those hard years before the war."

"Salazar has not told me about this. I'm very glad you think well of Victor Marriner, as I admire his paintings."

"I have four Marriners at my office, too. There were gifts from Victor himself."

Neil felt that Procopio's conversation was intended to lead somewhere else, somewhere less general and more specific. He wondered if the old man held resentment instead of respect for Victor Marriner. To have one's family name excised from the family house was not easy, even if a fair price was paid. Continuity of land and name meant a great deal in Santa Fe, so did the change to a new, thin-walled house on the north side come with grudges, nurtured through a generation?

"Mister Ortega, was your brother married? Did he leave children?"

"He was Salazar's age when he was killed, and he probably would not have married, as much as father wanted him to. He was in love with art. He showed great promise, but that was all cut short."

"But Salazar has come back."

"I was afraid he would want to leave us for New York or Paris. He says not, but I see many unknowns in his future. I, naturally, like my father for Placido, wish he would marry and stay here, fill the full promise of the Ortega clan."

Neil said, "Yes. I'm sure you do."

Salazar was seated at the far end of the table with Segunda and the elegant, older woman who greeted them. Neil noted that Salazar was the beloved son in this family as they all listened to him as he held forth. The heads at his end of the table turned to him with approving looks, loving looks. As he talked, he turned his eyes often to his father and Neil. After several minutes of their exchange out of his earshot, he got up and walked to stand behind Procopio's chair.

"What have you two been talking so earnestly about?"

"You, Salazar," Neil said.

"And...."

"Your father just said he wishes you would marry and stay here."

"Ah, who did you have in mind, Father?"

"There are many young ladies in Santa Fe. Your sister has a good friend who has waited for you, the Martinez daughter. She teaches school now and is a devout Catholic."

"We'll see. The Ortegas already have many branches, like an old cottonwood, so I think I'm really off the hook. One branch won't be missed."

"Not the way I see it, Salazar. All sons have that obligation to create another generation. But, this is a festive day, not for such serious talk."

Procopio's end of the table did not return to that subject for the rest of the evening. Salazar rescued Neil from his inquisition seat and they talked to cousins and aunts. Segunda held her own with a group of unmarried cousins. Procopio was at the door as they left.

"Mister Bronson, forgive me for asking. I knew Richard Marriner and heard of his death. How is Louisa taking his loss?"

"As well as could be expected, Mister Ortega. Estate tax problems have come to the fore, but she is hoping for a solution. There are large taxes this time, unlike when Victor died. "

"I'm sorry. Now she has no family left. I will write her a letter."

"She would like that, I'm sure."

# 24

# First Covering

For the whole month of March, after the last field trip of each afternoon, Neil retreated to Victor's studio to take on the completion of the Marriner paintings. Neil and Louisa agreed that he would not be paid for this work, as that implied a business relationship between them. He would put the last touches on as many paintings as he could in that month and it would be a project known only to him, Louisa and Lionel.

At the outset, Neil felt awkward in the old man's workplace, an intruder on his life and legacy. He started with the easiest pictures first, ones where only a portion of the sky was lacking or a patch of grass in the foreground to be fine-tuned. By the end of the first week, he had pulled together five paintings. The paints and mediums from Victor's cabinets were more buttery, smoother than what he was used to even after such a long time. Their oily nature intimidated him and he was forced to scrape off or wipe away whole sections. Then, he found he could assume the bravura of the older man's technique, a finishing stroke without hesitation. He imagined himself as a young Victor, bold and brash, attacking a canvas with brushes at arm length, the *bella figura* of artists in the past.

His work became bolder in the second week. He moved on to several paintings that had small portions of the work missing along the bottom of the canvas; for these, he consulted published photographs of other Marriner work. He must be careful not to inject his own ideas, but only use variations of the rightful originator. That approach worked well, and in the second week he finished ten more.

Sam, by then, had noted his disappearance in the late afternoon and asked him, "What's going on, Neil? I can never find you at the end of the day. Where do you go? Are you and Salazar spending a lot of time together?"

"No. I wish that's what it was, however. In truth, I've offered to help Louisa with some estate matters and it's taking more time than I anticipated."

"Maybe I can help you sometime. What sort of work is it?"

"Drudgery, mostly. Victor's letters and sketches. But, no thanks, Sam. I promised Louisa I would keep it all to myself; she feels it must be confidential at this stage. Not secret from you, but from the world of the Overtons and estate taxes."

"I knew you were pulling away from me, and didn't know what it was. I thought it was me, that I had done something, said something. I'll be glad when you're done."

"I think I am learning a bit about the old Victor Marriner, the way he did things. That shouldn't make all this work a complete waste. It won't be much longer."

"Good. I miss our afternoon glass of wine. I miss you."

The last group of paintings presented an assortment of deficiencies. Several had everything but a sky, blank canvas above a terrestrial finish. Another group sported a blank lower right corner, convincing Neil that the left-handed Victor must have started in the upper left corner and worked down diagonally to finish at the right bottom. It would be impossible for a right-handed painter to fake a Marriner, so Neil took being left-handed as a blessing for the first time, instead of the impediment it had often been in his youth.

Victor occasionally skipped over an object in the middle of a canvas, no doubt intending to come back to work on that when he was in a better mood. Neil understood this, having done exactly the same on his Galisteo paintings when a pinon or juniper in the middle seemed not worth the effort.

Neil soon mastered Victor's brush-stroke: a long, narrow rectangle, slightly curving, used for sky, ground or foliage, in varying sizes and combinations. He carefully built up the empty sections, stroke upon stroke, until it matched, in his eyes, what was already there. This was the largest group of paintings and Neil finished the last one on the last day of the month. Total: thirty paintings. He leaned them against the wall in a long line around the room. A couple of them looked awkward and obviously worked upon, but his objectivity had vanished. He would let Louisa spot those.

When she came in on the last day, she walked slowly around, picking up each canvas in turn to get a close look. She culled out three and put them aside. They weren't the same ones that Neil had questions about, so he kept his own counsel.

"The auction is not until mid-summer, so I will leave these in the sun by the windows to dry thoroughly. They are beautiful, Neil. You have summoned Father from the netherworld. I feel strangely like a long time ago when he was still alive and working. He would invite me into his studio when a painting was done and we would look at it together."

"Did you comment or advise?"

"Always. I was a bossy little girl and he played on that. On a few occasions he actually listened and did what I suggested."

"I can't think that you were a bossy girl. When must these be photographed for the auction house catalog?"

"Not until the end of June. It will then take a month or so to produce the catalog. I offered to write the descriptions for each entry, so none of the auction people need come here until then."

"That should give them plenty of time to really dry. The spirit of Victor is still in the studio, so let's hope they also have time to absorb it."

With Louisa's project behind him, Neil looked forward to a month of painting his own work, both in the studio and on his daily sorties to the countryside. He had built up a considerable pile of paintings from the classes outdoors. His large canvas series was advancing at a slower pace, but he had finished three of them and a new one was on the easel.

It was good to be in his own studio again. The long lines of the Galisteo Basin canvases were a soothing change from the close details of both his own *plein air* work and Victor's. Sometimes the smaller paintings seemed like needlework to Neil, painfully obsessed with detail. The new paintings had a grace and quietness that none of the smaller pieces could muster.

These larger panels were like unproblematic old friends, neither asking favors nor demanding changes. Almost as a way of admitting that the Marriner work was behind him, his energy burgeoned for his own canvases. A larger brush let him block in the basic forms on the composition and just as the sun was setting, he had the canvas with its first covering of paint. Some of it would still remain on the finished work, but many portions he would recolor with lighter shades or redraw with a different curved line. The first covering of paint, all of the pristine white under new paint, was a great jump forward in the finish of a painting: the first time it had form of its own, a life brought into the world.

Sam saw it the minute he walked in. "Wow. You ought to take time off more often. I like it. "

"Me, too. Let's have our glass of wine."

# 25

# Cascading Water

It was now early April and the *plein air* class was staked out along the Santa Fe river where the willows were green and grasses tumbled down the hills. Pale green mouse-ears were pushing out on the small trees. Spring brought a rush of water down the river and over the small cascade that Neil chose for his students. Although the water was murky, brownish from the accumulated silt of the winter, with the sun at its back, it transformed into white and pure. This was the *contra jour* technique that Neil discussed with them, looking back into the light to wash away strong colors.

The pattern of their classes were now deeply cut, each student going further into their exploration of landscape painting. They had completed sixteen new paintings, twice that number for those in their second semester. Neil was afraid to bask too much in their progress, this being his first year as an instructor, but he was amazed at how they had progressed. The ones that were truly motivated had gone further, now concerned with small matters of paintwork as well as the grand composition. They were well on the way to becoming accomplished painters, if not adult artists. Art could be taught.

Segunda continued her depressed, black-dominated versions of every scene Neil offered her, even this gurgling spring day came up in grays and dark browns. The water crashed over the rocks in leaden curves, grasses were so faintly green that they looked pale and chlorotic. Since her gloominess was not an act, but came truly from inside, Neil was able to hold back annoyance. Probably all her life would be seen through these dark lenses, bringing down the optimistic mate she would inevitably find. The gloomy always find the cheery, Neil thought, with sympathy for the young man who awaited. Your bride has decided to wear black to the altar, my boy, your wishes or those of her friends ignored.

"Nice and dark, Segunda."

"Thank you, Mister Bronson."

"You might try mixing a black from Ultramarine and Burnt Umber. It has a warm, hellish overtone, unlike the bluish cast of Carbon Black."

"I'll try those tomorrow."

Ollie was maturing into a fine young painter. His landscapes telescoped the whole view that Neil offered him, pulling the trees down and the water up, the peripheral sides of the scene came in without artifice. He could distill a complicated scene into the simple elements, and he often surprised Neil with his natural insight. He truly saw what he was painting. Won't the brothers back in Kansas be unhappy? No failed art school dropout to drive the tractor anymore, to sit on the porch with his siblings. He was headed for the Bigtime, wherever the Broadway of Art was.

"What prompted you to put those orange shadows against the grasses, Ollie?"

"I dreamed about that, Mister Bronson. I wanted to see if it would really work."

"It seems to very well."

Salazar had been watching him with the others, the three he talked to as he made his way to the left end of the crescent, the place Salazar always preferred. The painting on his easel showed an equal growth to Ollie's, but in a totally different direction. Salazar now saw all scenes broken into slabs, *tranches*, or splinters. It was if he had painted the scene on a sheet of glass, then carefully broken it into long spears and slightly rearranged it. That he could do water, cascading water this way was all to his credit. Neil thought he might be adapting the Descending Nude to a waterside scene, a subtle reference to that breakthrough painting.

"If I say brilliant, will you be in a bad mood with me?"

"No. Really?"

"I think it works and it could have been very forced, very self-conscious. You've taken the Marin and Victor Higgins technique and moved on with it. Brilliant."

"You not saying that just because you want me, are you?" he said softly with a smile.

"Of course. The powerful professor, bulging with hormones, will do his best to turn the head of the pliant, red-haired student."

"Now, I'll never know the truth."

"It's over-rated."

"Am I talking too loud?"

"Yes. The others all know, they're looking our way."

"Well, screw them."

The easiness with Salazar had grown and grown in the past month, the most open and loving he had ever been with anybody. Neil was afraid it would end, that the authorities would race up with blinking lights and put an end to it.

Salazar had wanted to know where Neil went every afternoon, too, and supposed he was spending it with Sam. Neil told him the same story, only slightly bending the truth that he has helping Louisa with estate matters. Neither of the men actually believed him, but they accepted it.

Salazar complained that he never saw him personally anymore, only as teacher and student. Neil wrapped himself in the long cloak of higher purpose, helping out a defenseless woman, a dear friend, who was being treated poorly. A few weeks, only, he said.

Salazar asked, "Are you really through with the work for Louisa?"

"Yes, all wrapped up yesterday."

"Can I come by your studio this afternoon?"

"You will get an F if you don't."

"What time?"

"Three. Sam is busy with the Studio Class until five."

# 26

# To Dance with the Devil

During the next week, Neil saw who he presumed was Gilbert Overton walking around the grounds of Casa Marriner on several occasions. Louisa's description of him as an "invasive bear" was all that was needed for Neil to recognize him. On his third appearance it was late afternoon. He was walking just outside of the studio window. Neil went outside to talk to the invader.

"You must be Gilbert Overton. I'm Neil Bronson, one of the instructors."

"Yes, you're Lionel's nephew."

"I understand you've made an offer to buy an interest in Casa Marriner. I've seen you here several times this week. Didn't Louisa give you a proper tour?"

"I'm trying to get a feel for the fine points of the property. Randolph Eisenhart was to give me a personal tour, but he is running late. This is the Roman Studio, isn't it? Would you mind if I saw inside, just in case the offer is accepted?"

"I suppose so," Neil said.

They walked into the large room and Overton whistled softly. "It's bigger than it looks on the outside. Old Marriner had a good eye for design, as well as for painting. I was just in the Moroccan Studio and the small casita behind it, both very impressive buildings."

"This is a handsome room."

Overton walked to the end and looked back. "How many buildings are there in total?"

"I don't know."

"Are there any plumbing problems? Electrical failures?"

Neil felt his patience and courtesy had come to an end. "I'm sorry I must go now, Mister Overton." He ushered Overton out, locked the door and walked past him away towards the main building. Lionel and Louisa were talking in the main hall when he entered.

"I just talked to Overton. He's snooping around."

Lionel said, "We saw him earlier. We're afraid we may be forced to do business with him."

Louisa looked at Neil with concern and said, "Lionel insists we stop our plans to auction the paintings you worked on. We might get good prices for them, but then lose Casa Marriner in a later investigation."

Lionel picked up the thread. "I'm very sorry, Neil. The work you did blends seamlessly with Victor's original painting. I am almost aghast at the facility with which you were able to forge his technique. Is there a criminal strain in the family I have not seen before?"

Neil smiled. "I just told myself it was an exercise in control and technique. Since I took no money personally for the work, it seemed there was no intent to defraud."

"The fraud would be on Louisa's part, and by extension, that of the Monmouth School," Lionel said.

"I am actually relieved. The ethics of it were always a worry to me. I can say I learned a lot, so the time was not wasted. I had a good time with Victor, like a long trip with somebody who became a dear friend and mentor."

Louisa said, "I shall always be grateful, Neil."

Lionel said, looking at Louisa, "I think we can include Neil in our discussion of terms we must present to this Overton, don't you?" She nodded, and he continued, "Until we actually do accept his offer, we have considerable bargaining power. I would ask that Eisenhart be retained only at his present instructor level with no special powers. The school itself will continue on exactly the same course, no changes. We will try to sell only forty-nine percent, just to keep a hand on things. Mister Wilson thinks that Overton may accept, the value is so great. Also, we would ask for eight hundred thousand. It seems like a dance with the devil, my dear, so let's brush up on our steps."

Neil said, "When are the inheritance taxes in fact due?"

She said, "The end of July. Mister Wilson calculates them now at five-hundred fifty thousand."

"Why don't you wait a while longer before accepting Overton? It may be Pollyanna-like to think something else will turn up, but if it does and you've already sold, you will be sorry," Neil said. "That's four months away. So let's just wait."

Louisa replied, "Is there a possibility that Overton will pull out if we wait? Loosing three hens trying to catch four?"

Lionel said, "Overton will not lose interest, by my reading. He has that grasping wife, Apricot, and the threat of no happiness at home should he not succeed. Perhaps Neil is right, we should just wait a while longer."

Louisa said, "So it's settled, then. We wait. I will write Overton, thanking him for his kind offer, but stating that the earliest I could make a decision would be the first of July. That should keep him on the hook."

When Neil got back to his studio, Sam was at work on his series of striped paintings at the far end of the room. The unstretched canvas was now stapled flat to the wall. The stripes were no longer just perpendicular to the canvas edge, but angled strongly across the space. Sam used bolder colors for his stripes, the painting on the wall in a range of pale yellows interspersed with deep cadmium yellows.

"It's all coming together, isn't it?" Neil said.

"It feels like it. I may have to throw away those first attempts, but I know I'm on the right track now."

"Did you see Overton walking around?"

"Yes. He asked to see our studio so I let him in. He's a nosy bastard, even looked into the closets."

"How long did he stay?"

"About five minutes. I finally asked him to leave."

"So did I, before you got here."

"You know, if bad manners and a relentless push make for success, I'm afraid he's going to succeed."

"Lionel and Louisa are already planning their negotiations with him. I'm hoping something else, someone else will show up."

"Let's hope so."

"Did you remember that we are due over at Carrie's now, to take Nicole out to dinner? Carrie told us she was arriving today."

"I know, I'm sort of dreading it. Speaking of determined, pushy people, there's one. Nicole. She heard that Carrie agreed to marry me and has come all this way just to make trouble."

"I don't think you have anything to worry about, Sam."

# 27

# Under the Tortilla

As Neil and Sam walked up to Carrie's casita, they could see through the window the two women sitting together on the day bed. A fire in the corner hearth made the room cozy and inviting, but Sam grumbled as he knocked.

It was Nicole who answered the door. "Ah, Sam. The lucky fiancé. And Neil, how good to see you. Come in."

Carrie said, still seated, "Now let me state some ground rules. Nicole is here for only several days, so both of you are on your best behavior. You can be pleasant for a few days, can't you?"

Neil said, "Definitely. So, Nicole, what do you think of our Santa Fe?"

"I have only been on the road from the airport to here. It looks like Fez rather than Marrakech to me. Brown houses with small windows. I can't see why you like it here when Morocco has so much more *panache.*"

"Perhaps we can arrange a lecture for you at the museum."

Nicole ignored him. "I was just inviting Carrie to spend the summer again in the Vaucluse at the auberge. She can forget the ties that bind and be herself again."

Sam said, "Carrie might be otherwise engaged this summer." He raised his eyebrows to Carrie and sat beside her at the space vacated by Nicole.

Neil asked, "Nicole, do the paintings we traded for your rent still please you?"

"Very well. I have had two offers to buy them, at quite an increase in price."

"You should sell. Be done with us," Sam said.

"I was tempted, but Carrie has talked me down. She believes you two will take New York by storm. If I wait a few years, I can build a whole new wing on the auberge with the proceeds."

He said, "Anything is possible."

Carrie drove them all to a downtown restaurant, where she had reserved a table by a far fireplace. Nicole picked at the enchilada that Carrie ordered especially for her, looking under the tortilla for anything more promising that lay below. It was quite unlike the refined product of her two-star chef back in Gordes. Carrie had the wisdom to order a French wine and Nicole checked the label, approved of it with a nod before allowing the waiter to pour. There was bottled water from France, as well.

Carrie said, "Everything about Santa Fe is an acquired taste, Nicole. The architecture, the food, the people, the clothes all are a singular life style. It appeals to Americans who have had too much of urban ways, as it appears to be simple and native. In truth, it is complex and sophisticated."

Nicole nodded and smiled at her. "I maybe need more time." She took a large gulp of wine.

"The chile peppers aren't too hot for you, are they?" Carrie said.

"I am on fire. How can you eat such things?"

"Again, an acquired taste."

"Enough of Santa Fe pleasantries. Nicole, what do you think of Carrie and Sam's upcoming marriage?" Neil asked, putting his thoughts on the table.

"I've told Carrie already. It is a vast mistake." His ruse got immediate results.

"Why do you think that?"

"Because she does not love Sam, at least not enough. He may love her, but she does not know her own mind."

Neil said, "And you know it better than she does?"

"Yes. She is too close to see it. Carrie has many parts. One loves Neil, one maybe will love Sam, and one loves me," Nicole said and put her chin up, awaiting attack.

Carrie said, "Nicole, I do love you and Neil, and I will love Sam completely, I know. His love for me is very strong and won't be bent out of shape by my treasuring others. There is a deep, male power in Sam, one that

I can rest on when I grow tired. Neither you, Neil, nor you, Nicole, have that. It does not mean that I don't love you as well."

Neil knew that Carrie was right. Sam's quiet energy was a source of refuge and solace for him, too. He said, "What do you think of that, Nicole?"

She answered, "The French see matters of the heart more clearly, just like we cook better than others. As regards the three of you, it would sound better in French, but here it is in English: She loves him, but he doesn't love her since he loves another him, but the second him in turn loves her, who doesn't return it, because she still loves the first him."

Neil said, "Bravo, Nicole. The French do see more clearly and that was a symphony on the mysteries of the English pronoun."

Sam frowned and asked, "But who is the other him?"

Neil said, "It's you, Sam."

He answered, "I'm getting dizzy, now. Where does Salazar fit in?"

Nicole asked, "Who is this Salazar?"

Carrie said, "He's a third him, but we don't have enough time tonight, Nicole. I will explain tomorrow."

Sam wanted to play with bait some more and said, "Nicole, Carrie tells me that she wants you to come to the wedding. In New York."

"I will be there. There is time between now and then, and miracles can happen."

"Like what?"

"Carrie will have an attack of sense, disease could kill all the men in Santa Fe, or the groom could change his mind, find a fat dancing girl with enormous breasts. Miracles happen all the time."

"Do you pray for them, Nicole?"

"I will start tonight. My father said it was never too late. One good Christian can make things happen."

# 28

## Scarlet Bands

Later in the week Nicole drove her rented convertible to Taos for the day and the daily patterns at the Monmouth School returned to normal. Both Sam and Neil were spending more hours in their studio, often late into the night.

Carrie found ways to be involved in the studio work of her two men. She brought by dinners that she personally cooked or arranged for takeout from local restaurants, giving them a break for an evening meal. When she asked if she could read aloud from the New York art magazines while they worked, they quickly agreed.

"Louisa is a fund of information," she said. "In the cigar factories of Havana, there were employees who did nothing but read Dickens aloud to the women rolling cigars. It was usually a man, an older man in a waistcoat and black tie. He sat high on a Hitchcock chair in the middle of the table where the women rolled, intoning *The Pickwick Papers* in Spanish translation. It's a charming image, Dickens's words wafting around amid the aroma of Cuban cigars."

"So why aren't you reading us Dickens instead of articles from art magazines?" Neil asked.

"I will bring *Great Expectations* tomorrow. It should last us until summer."

"And don't forget *The Tale of Two Cities*. I still shiver at the image of Madame de Farge knitting while the aristocrats lost their heads. Or *Bleak House*, quite appropriate for our inheritance dilemmas."

She said, "I am sure the girls did not have the right to request this or that, like a literary cafeteria. 'Please, Senor Garcia y Vega, read some Balzac to us today. Or can we have Proust tomorrow?' I alone will choose the reading matter."

Neil rolled along on his series of Galisteo River paintings. They had become more non-objective and abstracted with a barely discernible horizon and many undecipherable patterns in the foreground. The pinons and chamisa, so lovingly rendered in the *plein air* paintings, were now only reminiscent shapes, shading and contouring forgotten. The colors remained the natural earth colors of Galisteo, bright burnt siennas and ochres, greens changing from deepest black-green to pale blue-green, in many varirations. He accentuated the broad forms with thin lines of pure color, often a bright cadmium red or orange. Loose patches of paint dripped to the bottom of the canvas and the raw canvas showed through many of his finished compositions.

As with many painters who spend time in New Mexico, the color in both men's paintings had grown in intensity. Sam's banded paintings grew bolder and bolder, now all of them in shades of crimson or vermilion, an oriental overtone to the series. The stack of finished work built up in the corner, seven foot rolls waiting to be stretched.

# 29

# Fair Price

After one afternoon field trip, Neil returned to his studio to finish the painting that was on his easel. This was the part of the process that most appealed to him, the final touches that brought all the pieces together. These larger canvases demanded a different set of solutions from the *plein air* work. Instead of small lines of dark and light, he used bolder strokes and added opposing color where needed. It was close to a finish, when there was a knock at the door.

"Neil, may I come in?" Salazar asked.

"Certainly. You have a very serious look."

"It's nothing bad." He embraced Neil slowly, then stood back from him, holding his arms.

"I have something to ask Louisa, but I thought you might want to hear it first."

"What is it?"

"Father wants to make an offer for Casa Marriner. We talked about the problems with Overton and he said maybe it's time for the Ortegas to own their homestead again. He would buy it as a family trust, in all our names."

"I wonder if Louisa really wants to sell," Neil said, surprised.

"Father has sold some Ortega farm land outside of the city and needs to reinvest. He said he would do anything to make it work. Sale, lease, or whatever the terms."

"Louisa will be happy to hear that, I suppose."

"He wants to lease it back to the Monmouth School on a long term lease."

"Let's talk to Louisa right now." They quickly walked across the compound to the main house and through the reception rooms to her library office. She answered their knock.

"Come in. What brings you here?"

Salazar explained Procopio's offer. He would pay Louisa the appraised price that the lawyers for the estate had agreed upon. It was a fair price, Salazar said, and Victor Marriner had not quibbled about the Ortega's asking price so long ago. It was only right that he should return the favor.

Salazar was a bit hesitant when he said, "Father wants to give me the income. The deed would read Salazar Ortega Family Trust. The long lease will give me income for the rest of my life, he said."

Neil wondered if this was a maneuver to involve Salazar more deeply in Santa Fe. Procopio was weaving a kindly web, or at least it appeared kindly. Had he presented Salazar with provisos for this gift? If you marry this good, Catholic girl I will turn over great riches to you, my son.

Louisa said, "I must consult Lionel on this. I had hoped to keep the property in my name, but perhaps a long lease will serve the same purpose. I am disposed to accept it if I can receive assurances that Lionel and I can stay here the rest of our lives, lease or no lease. I would pick one of the houses for that assurance, big enough for both of us."

Salazar said, "As the expected owner, I can say yes to that."

"Let me call your father tomorrow with my answer."

Neil and Salazar left and walked slowly across the compound. The sun was setting and the Sangre de Cristos were a deep-orange. Neil wondered if this was the solution to the future of the school.

"If Louisa does accept, I want you stay on." Salazar said.

"You mean here, at the school another year?"

"Yes. To be honest, although I am giving credit to father, I was the one who came up with the idea to buy Casa Marriner. I thought it might convince you to stay with me in Santa Fe and not go to New York. I think father will let me live as I want, but I need to be in Santa Fe and I can't imagine life here without you."

"I've had my heart set on New York. You know that, Salazar."

"Maybe, stay on here just for a while. A couple of years or so. I feel if you go now I would never get you back."

"I am not sure you have me even if I stay."

"The chances are much better if you do; I can weave my magic blanket. Say yes, please." He kissed Neil a long kiss on the mouth, gently holding the back of his head. At first Neil was surprised, but then he returned Salazar's embrace.

Neil was stunned how excited the kiss made him. A tingle went from the back of his head where Salazar's hand held him, all the way down his back. It was what he had wanted from Sam but it had come from Salazar instead. He thought partly of Sam even now.

Neil realized that they were standing out in the open, in the middle of the main house parking. He placed his hand around Salazar's waist and led him back to the Roman Studio. He knew Sam was at Carrie' house for the evening, so they had the place to themselves.

He led Salazar to the bedroom and started undoing the buttons on Salazar's shirt. In a few seconds, they were both out of the clothes and in the bed. Neil saw that Salazar's tall body was slimmer, more vulnerable than he had expected. He felt a welling up of protection for him, a defenseless soul at risk in the wide world.

# 30

# Reversal

Procopio and Louisa met at the abstract office and signed the papers. Louisa would net more than enough to pay down the inheritance taxes and leave a handsome remainder in her account. Also in the pile of documents was a lease, a twenty-year lease, a length not seen before in the abstract office.

Procopio said, "It was almost fifty years ago that I sold this to your father. I am very glad it comes full circle now. And I must tell you, Louisa, that this is the easiest real estate closing I have ever been through."

"I've never been through one, but you made this all very accessible and agreeable, Procopio. Back again to the Ortega family."

"I never thought it would. Salazar was one who suggested it, and I immediately knew that it was the right thing to do."

"We can plan for next year at the school now. I can't wait to call Gilbert Overton."

Louisa left Procopio and walked across the street to her lawyer's office. Wilson had prepared the papers for the closing, including the many terms for the lease.

"Did everything go well at the closing?" he asked.

"Yes, thank you. But I have another matter to discuss with you."

# 31

# Domicile

It was spring day in New Mexico, windless, warm and air so clear you could see the mountain a hundred miles away. Neil had taken his class back to the Galisteo River site he was using in his own studio work. It never failed to excite him, the long rows of colors popping out in the dry, pellucid air. The students added to his enthusiasm and it was a good day of painting for all of them. Neil, himself, sketched in oil three versions of the scene in allotted time.

He thought about Salazar a great deal now. How would it work if he stayed on for a few more years? If his relationship with Salazar went sour, how could he continue in such a small town? No solutions presented themselves, only questions.

Salazar could see his concern as they painted. He said, "Your worried face is very transparent."

"I can't help it. There are so many unknowns just ahead."

"There are always unknowns ahead. It's called the future."

"Smart, but I'm a worry wart."

"Let's go out to dinner tonight. We can talk about it.

"All right. Pick me up at seven."

When he got back to his studio, Neil found a thick envelope stuck in the doors. He went inside and opened the letter from Louisa's lawyer; it said Louisa had requested him to produce and have registered a deed to show a change of property. He was now the owner of Richard's house on Patmos and its contents. All the attendant papers, stamped and recorded, were enclosed.

He took the papers and walked over to Louisa's library. Her door was open.

"Louisa, what is this?"

"A small thank you for the support you have given me in the last year."

"I did not expect a payment."

"I know. That is why it is so nice to give it, maybe as a surprise."

"It is a surprise."

"Richard's house could be a domicile for you, a refuge, a solace, the way it was for him. He often traveled elsewhere, but always felt Patmos was his center. It can be for you, too."

"I loved Patmos and don't know what to say. It feels awkward accepting this."

"Say nothing. It's already yours."

"Thank you. I will send your father's paintings back to you when I go there. They belong here."

"No, they belong there with you. I now have thirty newly-minted Victor Marriners to treasure here, you know." She smiled.

Neil kissed her on the cheek and walked over to his studio. Sam was working on his stripes and Neil told him about Louisa's gift.

"Although it's not exactly in the right location, it could be your house above the sea, Neil."

"I guess so. It is not at all how I had it pictured."

"It's very near the sea."

"And there is a supporting presence in the garden, under the fig tree."

"I've got some good news myself, Neil. The Larkin Gallery in New York has accepted my work from photographs for a solo exhibit this winter. What do you think of that?"

"It's all happening."

"Are you coming with us?"

"I don't think so, Sam. If I stay here, I can spend summers in Greece, and a visit with you and Carrie in New York on the way. Out painting today in Galisteo, I realized I have not finished with those long red escarpments. I may take years to complete what I have in mind. New York is just farther down the trail."

"I have an idea. It involves your new island house."

"I hope I know."

"Can Carrie and I come to stay with you this summer? After the wedding. I already have the paintings done for the exhibit. We can go through London and pick up our money from Hetty's show, travelers' checks in British pounds to spend on Patmos. A summer of swimming and nights in the taverna."

"I would love nothing better, if you can get along with Salazar. I'm sure he'll be there with me."

"Nothing's perfect, and I guess I have no right to be disagreeable."

"None whatsoever."

# 32

# Sensitive Nostrils

The summer evening was still hot, even though the sun had set and the sky was bright with remembrance. The islanders were just now looking around for a place to eat. Neil and Salazar sat at a table beside the harbor in Skala with a bottle of white retsina between them.

"I can teach you to swim better," Salazar said.

"I never was any good. I love the water, though, even if the sea doesn't love me back."

"The sea *is* good for you. That worry line in your forehead is gone and I can feel a muscle growing right there." He reached for Neil's upper arm.

"I'm sure there's a healing quality to salt water."

"You worked hard all year."

"Do you think we'll get bored here?"

"I doubt it. Are you bored now?"

"No. But I wonder how it will be for us to come here summer after summer. It's good to see Alicia again."

"I see why you are fond of her."

Neil looked out to sea and said, "She's the older sister I never had. I know she likes you, too. She said you had sensitive nostrils and a good thumb. Very important in a man."

"Carrie and your sweetheart, Sam, are due next week. Are you excited about their coming?"

"Somewhat. You aren't still out of joint about Sam and me?"

"No, but I love bringing him up and see how you react."

"Badly, I guess."

"Not badly, Neil, amusingly."

Neil said, "I didn't know when I asked them that we would be having such a good time together."

"There is a long line of people who love you, Neil. They probably all want to come to Patmos for a few weeks visit. Carrie, Sam, Segunda, Ollie, and your mother."

"I draw the line with Margaret."

"We've got other summers to be alone. Let's just do nothing but swim, eat and make love until they arrive."

"Suits me," Neil said, pouring more of the amber wine into each of their glasses.

This novel was printed on acid-free paper.
The typeface is ITC Clearface.